LATELY

BOOKS BY
SARA PRITCHARD

CRACKPOTS

LATELY

Sara Pritchard

LATELY

A Mariner Original

HOUGHTON MIFFLIN COMPANY

BOSTON • NEW YORK

2007

For information about permission to reproduce selections
from this book, write to Permissions, Houghton Mifflin Company,
215 Park Avenue South, New York, New York 10003.

Visit our Web site: www.houghtonmifflinbooks.com.

Library of Congress Cataloging-in-Publication Data
Pritchard, Sara.
Lately / Sara Pritchard.
p.   cm.
"A Mariner Original."
ISBN-13: 978-0-618-61004-4
ISBN-10: 0-618-61004-9
1. Northeastern States—Social life and
customs—Fiction. I. Title.
PS3616.R575L38 2006 813'.6—dc22
2006007127

Printed in the United States of America

Book design by Victoria Hartman

MP 10 9 8 7 6 5 4 3 2 1

Some of the stories in this book have been published—all in slightly different form—
in the following journals: *The Clackamas Literary Review:* "The Wonders of the
World"; *Northwest Review:* "The Honor of Your Presence" and "Late October, Early
April"; *Salt Hill:* "The Pink Motel"; and *Willow Review:* "The Christening." Thank
you to the editors of these journals for selecting my stories.

Lyrics: "Kookaburra," written by Marion Sinclair, year and copyright unknown.
"Don't Think Twice, It's All Right," words and music by Bob Dylan, copyright © 1963
by Warner Bros. Inc. Copyright renewed 1991 by Special Rider Music. All rights reserved. International copyright secured. Reprinted by permission. "Lately," by Greg
Brown, © Hacklebarney Music. Used with permission from Greg Brown.

The Lorine Niedecker poem is used with permission from the University of California Press. Hats off to The Bard for lines from his tragedy *Hamlet, Prince of Denmark,*
and to Coleridge for the lines from *The Rime of the Ancient Mariner,* quoted in "The
Christening."

To Kevin Oderman and Gail Galloway Adams

That was long ago—
Do you still love me,
Or do you hate me?
I wouldn't know,
I haven't seen you lately.

— *Greg Brown, "Lately"*

Consider at the outset:
to be thin for thought
or thick cream blossomy

Many things are better
flavored with bacon

Sweet Life, My Love:
didn't you ever try
this delicacy—the marrow
in the bone?

And don't be afraid
to pour wine over cabbage

— *Lorine Niedecker (1903–1970)*

Note on Place

Cook County and the towns of Indian Creek, Indian Gap, Ashport, and their surrounding areas where these stories take place are imaginary. They're some other-dimension locale in the northeastern United States that is part Pennsylvania, part the Ohio River Valley, part New Jersey, part New York, and part northern West Virginia: a place I call New Northwest Pennsy-hi-o. Any character resemblance to real people is purely coincidental. From 1954 to 1967, Woody Guthrie, who suffered from Huntington's chorea, was in and out of Greystone Hospital in northern New Jersey. He died at Creedmoore State Hospital in Queens, New York, on October 3, 1967. Rest in peace, Woody Guthrie.

Contents

LATELY

A Winter's Tale

FULL MOON, FIRST SNOW sticking to the pavement like confectioners' sugar on a jelly doughnut. After midnight, snow-quiet, and Celeste walking right smack-dab down the middle of Little Indian Creek Road, making a track like a rip in a long roll of gauze bandage. She could hear a car engine or the scrape and ring of a snowplow a mile away, plenty of time to get off the road, onto the berm, she reasons, and here in the center she's safer than out on the edges, where the woods spread out deep and dark before the entrance to Johnson's Orchard, the housing development where she lives, two or so miles up ahead. Celeste isn't afraid of people anymore — not like she was when she was young and lived in the city — not out here on this cold December night. Just the wild things alarm her, like the deer that scared the bejesus out of her when it hit her car a few minutes ago.

She'd seen the buck standing way in front of her, in the middle of the road. She could still picture him. Big rack and heavy, dark body — too dark almost, it seemed, for a deer — dark and big like a centaur. He was captured in her headlights with his body in profile, his elegant head turned toward her, a perfect shoot-me pose like on the cover of *Sports Afield*. At the sight of him, Celeste stopped and turned off the headlights, remembering what Graham had told her that time they were driving through the Poconos soon after their wedding: turn off the headlights to break the hypnotic trance of a deer blinded by brightness.

Celeste lit a cigarette and waited a minute or so and then turned the headlights back on — all clear — and started out again, but she hadn't gone very far when: *thunk!* A deer (the same one?) hit the car, slamming against the hood. Its head smacked against the windshield right in front of Celeste's face, cracking the glass and making her scream. When it hit the car and landed on the hood, Celeste saw the deer's face in the moonlight — its big, terrified face. Its imploring eye, the size of a yoyo, winked slowly, like a doll's.

She slammed on the brakes. The car skidded. The deer turned and looked right at her before it slid off the hood, scraping its hooves on the bumper like fingernails on a blackboard and sort of kneeling against the fender with its head bowed and front legs awkwardly folded, as if saying its prayers.

Celeste thought she heard the poor thing moan. *Amen.*

It snorted and struggled to its feet and then ran off at an angle into the black woods, its white tail waving bye-bye like a mittened hand. Celeste wondered if now the deer was sitting alone some place under a tree, stunned, too, and if it had seen her face as she had seen its — if her own terrified face loomed distorted and hideous on the silver screen of its memory.

When she tried to drive away, a hissing-dragging-scraping sound stopped her. She rolled the window down and leaned out, but she couldn't see what was the matter. Snow was still falling, coming down steadily and heavily like in an animated Christmas movie. It was the only time Celeste had ever wished she had a cell phone, a thing she'd resisted adamantly. She always hated people with cell phones, all the private conversations rudely going on in public — in stores and checkout lines, on commuter trains and planes, in restaurants . . . everywhere. People laughing and chitchatting and arguing, talking about the most intimate things — relationships and yeast infections — and making the most annoying small talk, right within earshot of everyone. Had they no manners? And all the cell phone towers poking out of the landscape everywhere like cowlicks. She hated talking on the phone. Why would she want to carry one with her?

But now, on this snowy night, what a relief it would be to pull out a little toy-size telephone and call someone for help. But what good would it do? Whom would she call? She could call home, but Julian, her son, wouldn't be there. He'd be off somewhere with his friends, and if he was home he wouldn't answer. He'd be sleeping; that's all he did at home anymore. She could call her friend Bobbie, but Bobbie lived on the other side of Indian Lake. It would take her a half-hour to get there. Celeste could walk home before that. Was there really no one else? Was 911 — a three-digit number — her only savior?

When she finally found the flashlight under the passenger seat and got out to examine the damage, the first thing she saw was a big smear on the road as if the deer had tried to make a snow angel, and a few round drops of bright red blood scattered like a handful of change. At the top of the rise, Celeste stopped to catch her breath and light another cigarette. She peered down the road to see if the lights of her Civic were still in sight (no) and then looked down at her tracks in the yellow beam. There seemed to be some letters . . . a word? . . . there in her footprint. What? She leaned in closer.

ES . . . what?

ESPRIT. ESPRIT, her footprints said.

"Goddammit," she said out loud, smearing the footprints within reach with the toe of her boot. What a vulgar, sneaky marketing technique, Celeste thought, this branding of the sole. If she'd noticed the logo imprint on the bottom of her new boots, she'd never have bought them. She imagined herself breaking into the Esprit shoe factory like those radical feminists who broke into the Mattel factory in the seventies and replaced all the Talking Barbie voice boxes with the voice tapes from GI Joe.

"Let's take the beach head!" postoperative Barbie shouted in her authoritative baritone.

"I love your hair!" GI Joe squealed.

ESPRIT. SUCKS. Celeste's boots would say. Or maybe JESUS. SAVES. JESUS. SAVES. Ha-ha-ha! Tammy Faye Bakker boots. Seriously, though, why not something philosophical — CARPE on the left; DIEM on the right — or some lovely image? A snowflake, a ginkgo leaf, a Celtic cross. Or how about the lovely Chinese characters Julian had tattooed on his arm last year?

Celeste was startled when she first saw the tattoos. Julian had kept them concealed, but she spotted the black marks on his arm through a thin T-shirt one morning as he was going from the bathroom into his room. Her first thought: leeches. Then: melanoma. She never saw Julian anymore, she realized, when he was not fully dressed. For years now she'd seen him in nothing but baggy jeans and a T-shirt and a hooded sweatshirt over that. When Julian pulled up his sleeve at her request, Celeste was at first surprised and then suddenly disappointed that he'd never shown her the tattoos. For so many years she knew his little-boy body so well: every scar, every scab, every freckle, every slight imperfection — washing him in the tub every night with that washcloth mitten shaped like Bullwinkle. She'd do all the voices for him: Dudley Do-Right, Rocky the Flying Squirrel, Boris and Natasha. How Julian would giggle and hold his nose and go under the water, blowing bubbles. "Porpoise," she called him for years, "my little porpoise."

Why had he never shown her the tattoos? He'd had it done last year, he said. What did she care? It was his body, he said defensively, before she even had a chance to respond.

"What does it say?" Celeste asked. The characters were beautiful — indigo, almost black — and looked like they'd been painted with a Sumi-e brush. She wanted to touch them, put out her hand to touch them, then drew it back.

Julian pointed to the first character. "Danger," he said.

The character underneath — even more lovely — the one that looked like a jack pine next to a mountain, he said meant "opportunity." Together they meant "crisis."

Celeste was baffled. "Why do you want the word *crisis* tattooed on your body?" she asked. She was careful not to sound critical. She was just trying to understand. Weren't there more than a thousand Chinese characters? He could have chosen any one, any combination at all, any word. Why *crisis*?

"Why not?" Julian answered. "Why do people do anything? Why do you get up in the morning? Why do you read all the time? Why do you go to your stupid job?" Julian was not shouting, but his voice was reproachful, full of disdain. He turned quickly and stepped into his room, closing the door in Celeste's face and clicking the lock.

Celeste walked down the hall and into the bathroom. Two blue jays were fighting at the redwood bird feeder just outside the window, squawking and spreading their wings and tail-feathers like cheerleaders showing off their two-toned skirts in a herkie jump. Celeste looked at herself in the medicine cabinet mirror, searching her face for something familiar.

"Why do people do anything?" she repeated to the flat face in the mirror.

"There's just no reason to carry on," the face whispered back. This was its mantra, its standard reply to any inquiry Celeste made.

The blue jays squawked and fought and carried on some more.

From Julian's room, Janis Joplin's voice crescendoed, singing "Piece of My Heart," until it seemed to Celeste that the ghost of Janis Joplin was standing right next to her, screaming in her ear. She could almost smell the intoxicating cocktail of Jack Daniel's and patchouli, the Zippo's flame scorching the stainless steel spoon. The lyrics flung her back to her own youth — India prints and love beads and little cones of incense, pipes fashioned from aluminum foil, peace marches and draft card burnings, turntables spinning *Cheap Thrills, Are You Experienced, In-a-Gadda-da-Vida.*

That night in bed, after she'd first seen Julian's tattoos, Celeste lay awake for hours, tossing and turning in spite of the pill she'd taken, imagining what word she'd have tattooed on her own body, what summed it all up. At one point she came up with a Post-it note tattooed on her back bearing *Kick me* in a cartoonish font, or maybe a simple question mark tattooed on her forehead, a price tag on her toe with DRASTICALLY RE-DUCED in red boldface type. A bar code, like a stripe of war paint, on one cheek.

Why couldn't she be serious? Even in her darkest hours, when suicide came knocking at her door in its yellowed shirt and drab, ill-fitting suit, ringing the bell like a sugar-crazed trick-or-treater, even then, feeling so desperate, something about her was so nonchalant, so flippant, so devil-be-damned. She was nearly always, it seemed, so much more alive and brave in crisis situations than in everyday life.

It was a character flaw. A bad smart-ass gene. Embarrassingly enough, she'd even gone so far as to tell a joke at her husband's funeral. Not a joke-joke, just a tasteless anecdote about how her uncle had driven a U-Haul in her grandmother's funeral procession — from the funeral home right to the gravesite — so he could get back to the house lickety-split and snatch all the antiques and valuables while the rest of the heirs were still eating spiral-cut ham and tortellini at Madeleine's, licking their lips and anticipating the reading of the will.

Her own father, who had been appointed executor of the will, whispered to Celeste at the gravesite, "To the buzzards go the spoils." He nodded toward the U-Haul parked on the cemetery's narrow gravel path and laughed and never questioned, never confronted his brother regarding the ransacked, half-empty house they all returned to after the reception.

And as she told the story at Graham's funeral, Celeste couldn't stop laughing, recalling what that procession from years before must have looked like: the hearse, the limousines, the U-Haul, parading along Montauk Highway to the cemetery, their little funeral flag hood ornaments whapping in the wind. "National Lampoon's Death in the Family," Celeste called it, laughing and spilling her drink.

But at Graham's funeral, she was the only one laughing.

"I guess you had to be there," Celeste said, and laughed and burped and laughed some more.

Everyone was horrified. Julian was twelve then. He glared at his mother and shook his head. "Asshole," he swore under his breath. Graham's mother spit into her handkerchief and turned away. Unthinkable, crass, how Celeste had acted at her husband's funeral. Yes, she'd had a few drinks, and yes, she'd been taking the pills to get through it all, but still . . . she'd told the story because it was one of Graham's favorites. He loved Celeste's stories and how she could make people laugh. Time and time again, he'd say, "Celly, tell the one about . . ."

Had it really been seven years since Graham died? Almost twenty-six, then, since her own father passed away? And Miriam, her mother, poor Miriam. "Don't put me in a nursing home," she had pleaded. She'd said it for years, but there came a time when Celeste had to. She just had to. She couldn't do it anymore.

Maybe that's what Celeste should have tattooed on her body: TO THE BUZZARDS GO THE SPOILS. Or maybe the inscription her father had joked that he wanted for his tombstone: I TOLD YOU I DIDN'T FEEL SO GOOD — a joke or a final insult, Celeste wasn't certain — to the wife who always scolded, "Ach! Don't pay him any attention; he's a hypochondriac" when the poor man complained of any discomfort.

At any rate, shouldn't you try to be a bit original in death — and tattoos? How original was a butterfly? A rose? The cracked, puffy heart pierced with its little dart? But, say you loved the butterfly, the rose, the heart. Did it really matter at all how original you were in anything, especially, *especially* in death? Who would dare call a tombstone inscription — or a body tattoo — on charges of plagiarism?

Death, the great equalizer. Who said that? Tolstoy? Donne? Celeste's mind was racing. Or was it just a theme that replicated itself again and again like a seed crystal? Some universal pipe dream of eventual equality, ultimate justice, everlasting fairness, rendered with the reaper's annihilating swoop?

Maybe she'd just have the entire text of *The Iliad* tattooed on herself from head to toe. In one-point type. In the original Greek. Or better yet: DANGER OPPORTUNITY CRISIS, like Julian — like a coat of arms it would be — drawn in the beautiful, mysterious Chinese characters.

"DANGER, OPPORTUNITY, CRISIS, oh my! Danger, opportunity, crisis, oh my!" Celeste repeated the phrase over and over as she walked through the snow, like Dorothy and her entourage en route to Oz. Only Celeste was all alone, no skipping, no arms locked with a lion, a tin man, a scarecrow.

"Danger, opportunity, crisis, oh my!" In the deepening snow, Celeste's boots embossed their subtext: ESPRIT! ESPRIT! ESPRIT!

Far in the distance, a car engine raced and tires spun. Nearby, something crashed in the woods — animal, vegetable, or mineral, Celeste couldn't discern. From the direction of the old Johnson barn came the sound of someone whistling, a sweet melody Celeste couldn't quite place. Years ago, a young girl's body had been found in there, buried in the hayloft like a pretty egg in an Easter basket. A perfect body. Fully, neatly clothed. Not a mark on it. No indication of foul play. No cause of death, no motive, no murderer. As if the girl had just burrowed in there and died.

Celeste stopped and shined her light into the trees. Quickly something moved outside the hoop of brightness. Another crash and crunch. Was something or someone shadowing her there in the woods? Where once she would have frozen in fear or, easily startled, fled screaming, tonight Celeste did neither. She stepped toward the noise, across a narrow ditch, losing her footing for a second but grabbing on to a stout rhododendron branch for balance and pulling herself up. The flashlight tumbled and rolled a few feet away as Celeste climbed up the low, slippery embankment. Without the incandescent light, the woods shone eerily bright, like a high-contrast black-and-white infrared photograph. The vision was almost blinding, and in the starless sky the moon gleamed like a silver dollar in the palm of a black hand.

What a beautiful sight! What a beautiful night! Celeste stared into the woods, hypnotized by the beauty, big snowflakes falling all around her like confetti on New Year's Eve at Times Square. The trees, twisted and vine laden, some half-fallen and caught in the arms of others, looked a bit like gigantic letters, like an elaborate sylvan alphabet, an enchanted calligraphic forest where at any moment a letter-tree might yawn and stretch its limbs and begin reciting a silly poem or singing some nonsense song. Look: There was an ornate *W* right in front of her, an illuminated *P* leaning against it, a cursive *S* slouching next to that.

"I'd like to buy a vowel," Celeste called out into the woods and laughed. The sound of her laughter shimmered and tinkled in the cold air like a small glass ornament, a crystal hummingbird, say, a precious heirloom from a Victorian Christmas tree. Another noise. A snap. A crunch. A branch underfoot. Celeste didn't move.

The Lost Pilot

I n the airport limo, Jay removed his cap and rehearsed the
lie he would tell Sue Mai. He could say it now with ease, pausing
here and there to imagine her response and then continuing
on with another facet of the deception recited as rotely as the
Pledge of Allegiance. He could even convince himself — for the
ride's duration, at least — of the lie's veracity. In reality, Jay told
himself, the things he would tell Sue Mai *were* true. They were
all small truths, all related to the whole truth, which was
wrapped around that core of awkwardness and otherness that
had underlain his life for as long as he could remember, separat-
ing yet defining him. Nothing could pierce that core, dislodge
that truth, nothing could alter it. Jay was sparing Sue Mai by
breaking off the engagement.

He was set in his ways, he would tell her. That was the first
little truth. Past middle age, he would say (truth two). He did
not want the responsibility of a family (true). There was the nature of his work: the constant travel, the danger nowadays, the
stress and exhaustion (true). Weird hours and constant jet lag —

something he'd never been able to overcome, a condition as ironic as that of a sailor who suffers from seasickness. He did not get on well with other people on a social basis, Jay would explain. He'd always been a loner — an understatement, to say the least.

He was all work and no play, people said, yet the same people looked up to him. They felt safe when he was in charge. He was famous for his smooth landings, never the bump and bounce of the inexperienced and sloppy pilots. When he stood in the cockpit doorway as passengers disembarked, they always thanked him, many of them complimenting him, some of the older passengers placing a liver-spotted hand like a toad over his and smiling their dentured grins, smiles too big and bright for their diminished frames and faces.

Once on a flight from Frankfurt to D.C. on a 747, the landing gear would not descend, and Jay had to make an emergency landing on a special runway sprayed with fire-retardant foam, far from the Dulles International terminal. Fire trucks and emergency vehicles waited off to the side of the landing strip, and when Jay glided the plane in as smoothly as a puck on a shuffleboard, there was a profound silence, and then a deafening roar as everyone on board cheered. From the cockpit window, Jay could see the airport's emergency personnel throwing their hats up in the air and raising their arms in triumph. From the radio, the air traffic controllers could be heard cheering, and that evening when the passengers deplaned, many of them kissed him, throwing their arms around him and unabashedly crying, saying, "Bless you. God bless you, Captain. Peace. Shalom."

Later that night, he was the toast of the officers' club, and Ariel, the young tomboyish stewardess with whom he'd had a brief affair earlier that year, invited him to her room.

For weeks afterward, he received thank-you notes from the flight's passengers. One elderly woman sent him a fruitcake baked by Trappist monks in Berryville, Virginia; a rare first edition of Thomas Merton's *The Seven Storey Mountain* in its beautiful white cloth binding; and a prayer card from Naples, Italy, of Saint Joseph of Cupertino, known as the flying friar and the patron saint of pilots and aviators. From the prayer card, Jay learned that Saint Joseph of Cupertino's life was a series of visions and ecstasies, and that yelling, beating, pinching, burning, and even piercing with needles could not break his trances, during which he often levitated and floated about like a feather. Although neither religious nor superstitious, Jay folded the prayer card and tucked it inside the band of his pilot's cap.

HE HAD NO interests, Jay would tell Sue Mai, no hobbies anymore, no passions. He did not care for the movies even. Or nature, for that matter. And she was almost fifteen years his junior. He liked the boy, but he could not spend much time with him. He would not say that exactly, though, because it would sound cruel. The boy was sweet and good-natured, pretty as a little girl, with black eyes and the straight, black, shiny hair cut in a bowl, like the Vietnamese children he had known.

What kind of life would a wife of his have, anyway? Jay would point out, him being gone so much of the time. Everything crammed into a few days here and there. They should break it off now. The worry, too, in these times.

The absence of solitude, he thought to himself. That was it, but he would not say it. And all his things mingled with Sue Mai's, the ultimate loss of privacy. That was part of it. That would be too much.

There was all that. He would enumerate all that, but there was the other side of the coin: He cared about Sue Mai. He loved her. He loved her company, her quiet voice, and the way she doted on him. The small, exquisite meals she prepared: paper-thin slices of radishes and cucumbers curled like transparent blossoms on the dark, rectangular plates. He loved Sue Mai's beautiful manners, her fine features and smooth skin, her slim, childlike figure. The clothes she wore: silk blouses and soft cashmere sweaters, weightless almost. Simple, elegant jewelry: amber earrings small as the tapers' flames and thin silver bracelets that orbited her wrists like the rings of Saturn.

He loved her pale stockings and tailored skirts; her small, narrow shoes that fit in his hand like fairy boats — elaborately embroidered brocades or leather soft as lambskin against his cheek — their toes tipped and pointed, their heels stiff and substantial as bone. A cream-colored silk kimono with pale green fans and orange chrysanthemums on the outside — a splash of bright magenta halfway down the lining and rushing down each sleeve like a sore throat — hung on the back of the bathroom door and fluttered against his face when he closed the door behind him.

The boy was well behaved. He ate daintily with the inlaid ebony chopsticks, never clicking them together as Jay sometimes did so clumsily himself, so uncouthly — an ugly sound like the clacking of false teeth. There was a language, too, of chopsticks, he knew, an etiquette. One should never point with them when speaking or let them stand upright in a bowl of rice. What did it mean to let them click together? He wanted to ask but was ashamed, and Sue Mai and the boy averted their eyes every time his chopsticks slipped and clicked; they seemed embarrassed, as if he'd done something as crass as passing gas.

The boy spent every other week with his father and was really never any problem. He played quietly by himself and always asked politely to be excused from the table. He even bowed slightly when addressing Jay, lowering his eyes almost coyly it seemed, his black lashes, in the candlelight, casting a feathery shadow across his wide cheeks.

IT NEVER SHOULD have started — their seeing each other. Meeting in the lobby and the elevator, at first just hellos. Jay could not help but notice Sue Mai — so refined, so well dressed, so reserved, so small and feminine. It was only polite to nod, to speak. Then the cappuccinos at the Starbucks next door. The short walk to the jazz bar, the drinks. Brad Mehldau playing "Satin Doll" and "Angel Eyes." The light meals in her apartment, the flickering candles, the sensuous music: Nina Simone, Dave Brubeck. The warm, sweet sake, the laughing and telling stories about this and that. The places Jay had been: Germany, Italy, Spain, his tour in Vietnam.

Sometimes after dinner, the boy — Quinn was his name — sat on Sue Mai's lap on the long white couch, a raku vase of peacock feathers waving ever so slightly on the end table when one of them shifted their weight or gestured, or when the air conditioning clicked on. Quietly, in his stocking feet, Quinn brought Jay things to admire. Tiny origami birds and animals he had made: a crane, a swan, a cock, a hare. Quinn knelt at the glass coffee table as gracefully as a geisha attending at a tea ceremony, his feet tucked under his buttocks, and opened a vellum folder with the thin, bright papers — squares of golds and reds and purples, turquoise and yellow-green with black markings that resembled apostrophes and bird footprints.

The lights of the city blinked like a control panel behind him as step by step Quinn folded the paper carefully this way and that, creasing it with his perfect pink thumbnail, his hands smooth, fingers long, the color of fresh ginger. Every few minutes, the lights of a descending plane appeared in the tall glass windows, coming in for landing at LaGuardia, just beyond the river and the city. Jay even liked the little dog, a Boston terrier named Rumi, who sat by the low table while they ate, pretending not to be begging, looking away nonchalantly if he caught anyone looking at him, as if to give the impression that he could care less if a spring roll or a piece of spicy chicken found its way, intentionally or not, onto the floor.

There was all that, but Jay would still let Sue Mai go, like he had let Ariel and so many others. As the city's galaxy of lights spread before him, Jay dreamed. Out the limo's windows, he stared at the suspended streams of headlights and taillights arching over the dark waters of the East River, and the delicate necklace lights of the Brooklyn, Williamsburg, Manhattan, and Queensboro bridges. Sheet lightning flashed on and off as if a child were playing with a light switch, illuminating the sky-line for a split second then returning it to its *scherenschnitte* silhouette.

Jay recalled his first plane ride — at the Cook County fair-grounds when he was thirteen. His mother had paid for them to fly over the county in a four-seater Cessna. They sat in the back, the pilot and another boy, younger than Jay, up front. Jay's mother leaned across him, smelling of White Linen, and pointed out Indian Gap Mountain in the distance and Cook's Fort; the squiggly path of Little Indian Creek and the bedpan-shaped glimmer of Indian Lake; their farm, which embraced both and then spread out far beyond, toward the asylum and the river; and the Indian burial mound that rose up out of the land-scape like a velvety breast.

He looked down on hay fields and cow pastures, and he picked out the old Mail Pouch barn on Little Indian Creek Road, which dated back to the early nineteenth century, and the new cow barn, long and low with its shiny tin roof. His mother pointed out the hilltop with the Johnson family burial ground adjacent to a copse of beeches, his ancestors' bones sweetening the field below, and the two new housing developments with their split-level homes like the little plastic houses and hotels on a Monopoly board, lined up neatly where his grandfather's and his great-grandfather's pastures and orchards used to be.

He could still picture that ride. That feeling when they took off, that heavy feeling in the seat of his pants and then the lift, the rise, the leveling off, the joy, the new perspective, the exhila-ration of flying, Jay never forgot. That night in bed after his first flight, Jay felt that thrill again when he closed his eyes. From that very day so many years ago, Jay knew that he would fly, that he preferred to be suspended rather than grounded, looking down on the earth, on life, like a goose or a hawk. From the sky you could find your place on Earth, just as if you, too, were a token on a board game: shoe, cannon, thimble, iron, dog. In the sky, you were removed from the noise and confusion, the jeering boys and the silly, laughing girls, tossing their shiny ponytails, waving their polished fingernails, pursing their pink wet lips and calling you faggot, calling you Jane. Soon after that first plane ride, Jay began to study a set of books for the pilot's ground-school exam, books that had belonged to his uncle, and then he started checking out book after book on aviation from the Cook County library.

When he was a boy, Jay loved the outdoors at night, when the barn owls hooted and the crickets sang and the whippoorwills and catbirds called, and the lightning bugs made the night all glittery like the cards he received every Valentine's Day and Easter from his grandmother. By the time he was ten, he knew all the constellations and the names for each full moon, and all the moon lore and mythology: wolf moon, snow moon, worm moon, pink moon, flower moon, strawberry moon, buck moon, sturgeon moon, harvest moon, blood moon, beaver moon, cold moon.

He studied first the *Old Farmer's Almanac* and *Llewellyn's Moon Signs,* which his grandfather had farmed by: root crops planted in the dark of the moon, fruits and flowers and vegetables that bear crops above ground planted during the light of the moon, corn at the buck moon, animals bred during the pink or flower moons. Jay kept studying, moving on to other, more esoteric books on astronomy, astrology, and alchemy. In high school, he found great pleasure in the sciences: chemistry and physics — the universe of spinning atoms, the glory and spectacle of fire and bubbling concoctions, of physical and chemical changes that transformed matter in stunning and miraculous ways, the possibilities and probabilities of matter existing in the absence of time.

When he began flight training at sixteen, he continued to be awed by the lay of the land and the way that from the sky he could trace the routes he walked at night, making his way along the hem of woods along Little Indian Creek Road, just out of sight, and along the edges of the new, manicured lawns in Johnson's Orchard, where he could see in the yellow-bright windows of the new houses like open doors in an advent calendar — families sitting at their tables, saying grace, passing bowls; behind closed doors, arguing; sprawled on their couches in their dim rec rooms, illuminated by a television's flickering blue light; or in their bedrooms, dressing and undressing. But the people in the houses — some of them the same classmates who taunted him — couldn't see Jay obscured by the darkness just beyond the cozy rim of their private lives. When he walked, he carried with him the tiny mother-of-pearl opera glasses that had been his grandmother's. Some nights after walking, Jay returned home drenched and weak and exhausted, full of desire and drunk with visions and fantasies.

This was the late sixties, when the city dwellers were beginning their great exodus, the farmland turning its back on the pastoral, curtsying to suburbia, and Jay walked the cusp. In his lifetime, he would see it all transformed, except for a little woodlands here and there, buffer strips between housing developments and The Meadowlands golf course. The Beeches, Cowslip, Foxglove Estates, Johnson's Orchard, The Pines, the developments were called: mazes of culs-de-sac lined with modern houses, each development bigger than the one before it, yards clashing in bursts of exotic plants and swimming pools flashing water the color of windshield washer fluid. Today, Jay's mother's house — the old Johnson homestead — with its phlox and hollyhocks along the wall and its few remaining acres, looked as out of place on the landscape as an Amish buggy on the autobahn.

American farmland, it was apparent to Jay, was being gobbled up and gulped down by developers. The night sky was polluted with light spilling and spreading out from the cities like a terrible stain. He preferred the dark skies over the mountains and deserts, over great expanses of Africa and eastern Europe, over the dark seas.

Lately, as Jay flew the transatlantic flights, the waters and the earth seemed to come alive, to reveal themselves to him. History unveiled. Once on a flight from London, in a holding pattern while awaiting a runway at JFK, Jay saw the tall boats below, and in the Hudson Bay, the longboats filled with half-naked, paddling Indians. Soon afterward, crossing the Atlantic, he spotted the Spanish armada, and on another trip, the *Titanic*, half-sunken, glimmered in the moonlight, her prow sticking out of the water like a bird's beak, lifeboats scattered around her like popcorn, icebergs gleaming in the background. On another flight, over the Aegean, he saw, plain as day, Ulysses in rags, thrashing, lashed to the mast of his ship, the sirens singing and beating their wings about him.

And just this evening again, during a storm over the Atlantic, he saw the fire dancers on the wings — the women consumed in fire: fiery hair, fiery garments, twirling fiery batons — and as the passengers disembarked, he saw again the ghosts of American Airlines Flight 77, the blond woman and two small children, a whole line of people behind her, with their panicked faces and slack mouths. The blond woman held up the line as she always did, bending down in the aisle to tie one of the children's shoelaces.

The heavens were populated, Jay knew that. Lost pilots, lost crews, lost passengers, even the spirits of the drowned and the souls of those who'd never ventured from terra firma, roamed the firmament, fluttering about the planes like moths around a streetlamp, peering in the windows for relatives and loved ones left behind, tapping on the glass, waving, making faces. Twice now, his old friend Petrowski, another B-52 pilot, had floated up to the cockpit window and made a monkey face at him, stretching out his mouth at the corners with his index fingers and sticking out his tongue, flattening his nose against the windshield. The second time, Petrowski had Devron, his gunner, in tow, both of them laughing and clowning around outside the cockpit window. Devron took a long toke from a Thai stick and offered it to Jay, mouthing something while holding his breath, something Jay couldn't quite make out. Then the two of them receded into the blackness, laughing.

Through the cockpit window this evening, the night had reached in and touched him with its velvet gloves. The stars and planets had never blazed so brightly. Venus glowed white, Mars orange, like friendly buoys. Beyond, the black warplanes gave a spectacular show, flying all around him in the Blue Angels' diamond formation, swooping and turning in perfect synchronization, like flocks of starlings. They spoke to him in semaphore, silently guiding him. All his planes were there, too, just as he remembered them lining the shelves of his room in the old farmhouse, all the model planes he'd built and painted as a boy: the Messerschmitts and de Havillands; Condors and Wildcats; Shooting Stars, Hellcats, and Spitfires; Bearcats, Panthers, Cougars; even his favorite, the Grumman Goose.

Spirits did, they really did, fly up, and if you spent enough time up there — like Jay had — you could see them. He'd heard stories about this in flight school. Old pilot's disease or Saint-Exupery's syndrome it was called, or sometimes Jorgensen's dementia, after the Danish pilot who caused a commercial airline collision in the fifties by changing course to avoid hitting, he said, a band of angels "wide as the Milky Way." Sailors who had been at sea too long saw them, too — ships riding the air currents up and down like waves, denizens of the spirit world.

The public believed that some pilots retired young because of the superb physical condition their jobs demanded of them, that they retired because of failing eyesight — less than 20/20 vision — or poor reflexes, or sudden, inexplicable heart palpitations or high blood sugar. That was bullshit. Flying was all computerized nowadays, as if each plane were commanded by a boy on a beach aiming a remote control up into the white sky, and the pilots just sat there, crash dummies in splendid uniforms, staring into holy space for the duration of most flights, snapped into action by turbulence, emergencies, and landings.

The way of the world was, when you started to see things, they took you down.

There were other stories, too, about a gateway over the Atlantic, directly above the lost city of Atlantis, the lost continent of Mu, the southeastern tip of the Devil's Triangle — around latitude 25°N and longitude 85°W, and other places, too. Jay had read about these paranormal phenomena when he was a teenager. The gateways were indicated by a dazzling set of blue doors with jeweled silver hands as door knockers upon them. The doors were visible only on certain dates in certain places, in certain astrological and astronomical configurations — equinox, eclipse, harmonic convergence, syzygy — and if you flew straight into them from just the right angle, they flew open — just like in *Ali Baba and the Forty Thieves — Open, Sesame!* — and you would enter and orbit forever in this slim, immense pocket of timelessness and pure space.

Jay had first seen the blue doors while flying a B-52 over Cambodia during the war — the American War, Sue Mai called it, because that was how her parents always referred to it. But Jay was stoned then and he kept going; it was the only way he could do it. Three years ago, though, he saw the blue doors again, and when he saw them once more, he knew his fate was sealed, just as his life had been claimed by that first airplane ride with his mother on a muggy August afternoon in 1963 at the Cook County Fair. There were things like this in everyone's life — touchstones, turning points, irreversible choices, sudden veers and reversals, snap decisions, monumental — unheard-of — life-altering changes at the very last second: a bomb dropped, a girl in a pink fuzzy sweater screaming.

The blue doors, for Jay, were the obvious, the only and ultimate conclusion. He would disappear through them. For now, he would tell the limo driver to turn around, send a message by courier to Sue Mai, the lie no longer a lie, the truth so clear: he simply couldn't continue his masquerade with her. Then on with his life and just wait. Next time, when the circumstances — the dates and numbers and planets — were just right, he would be ready, he would resist not, nor hesitate, falter not, nor reconcile, nor repeat. He would alter the course of his life. He would turn off the controls and unplug his ears and let the sirens sing; take off his hat and let Saint Joseph of Cupertino guide him; close his eyes and let the Blue Angels escort him all the way down, all the way down to zero.

Late October, Early April

DURING THE FIRST TRIMESTER, Alma was so sick she couldn't keep anything down. Even a tiny oyster cracker or a little sip of ginger ale made her vomit. She was so sick she lost twelve pounds, and when she went to the doctor, he said, "Alma, this is serious dehydration, dangerous to you and your baby," and he put her in St. Anthony's on an IV to replenish fluids and restore lost electrolytes so she could get her strength back. Two days later he said she could go home, and he wrote her a prescription for thalidomide, which he said would prevent any further problems with nausea and vomiting.

Alma can still recall that day so vividly: sitting on the bed in St. Anthony's Hospital thirty-eight years ago in her box-pleated skirt and polka-dot blouse, her navy blue raincoat with the zip-in/zip-out lining folded neatly on her lap, her straw purse on top of that. Raymie, she says, was wearing his Coca-Cola bottling plant jacket and sitting in a squeaky vinyl chair against the wall, twirling his rabbit's foot keychain while old Dr. Elsworth talked and tore the prescription off his pad. It was late October, and outside the hospital window a handful of white sycamores and the orange roof of Howard Johnson's tried to make something interesting out of the drab landscape, but whatever their intention, the effort was lost on the people in the hospital room.

"Eat anything and everything you want now, Alma," Dr. Elsworth said. "You have a lot of catching up to do. Take one of these three times a day and everything will stay down."

And he was right, too. On the way home, Alma and Raymie stopped at Howard Johnson's and had milkshakes, fried clams, French fries, and coleslaw, and Alma ate like a horse, even ordering rice pudding for dessert, which arrived in a sundae glass with a dunce cap of whipped cream and a maraschino cherry on top. It was a Friday, a payday, and Raymie put his arm around Alma in the turquoise booth and said, "Honey, I've never seen you eat so much."

Alma must have been half-starved, and then she gained almost seventy pounds by the time Jude was born.

ALMA'S MOTHER WAS a Catholic. "The Lord works in mysterious ways, Alma," she said to her daughter, but neither one of them could keep from crying when they looked at the baby. Had Jude been a girl, he was to have been named Irene Rose after Alma's mother and Raymie's oldest sister. Alma and Raymie had planned to name a boy Raymond Harry, Jr., but when they saw the baby, it somehow did not seem proper to name him after Raymie.

"You pick a name," Raymie said to Alma and went out into the waiting room to smoke a cigarette, and so Alma picked the name Jude, after Saint Jude Thaddeus, faithful intercessor of those in need, patron saint of hospitals and desperate causes, maker of miracles.

In her jewelry box, Alma kept a Saint Jude Thaddeus prayer card with a pewter pendant attached. Saint Jude, who Alma thought looked like Raymie, was depicted with a little flame like that of a cigarette lighter's over his head and holding a medallion of Jesus — big as a hubcap — in front of him. On the back of the prayer card was the "Don't Give Up" prayer that Alma used to read almost every Sunday night when she had a lot of homework due on Monday that she hadn't even begun and couldn't possibly finish by the next morning. She'd taken advantage of Saint Jude's power and mercy to help her solve some quadratic equations and finish reading *Great Expectations;* would he find it in his heart now to intercede and fix her baby? *Just this one miracle,* she prayed to Saint Jude. *Just this one.*

Two maiden great-aunts, Aunt Rosewetha and Aunt Phoebe, the postmistress, sat in the waiting room, too, as Raymie smoked his Kool. "We must all bear His cross," Aunt Rosewetha said, speaking metaphorically, and Aunt Phoebe sniffled and nodded in agreement, dabbing at her eyes, like she often did, with a folded hankie, a little brown dog neatly cross-stitched on one corner.

BERYL ANN, ALMA'S little sister, had just turned thirteen then, and she spent every free moment with Baby Jude. She scooped him up out of his crib and cuddled him, changed his diapers and gave him his bottle, fed him strained apricots and Gerber's rice cereal from a curved spoon with a tiny Alice in Wonderland on its handle and the Mad Hatter etched in its bowl. She rocked him on the porch swing and bounced him and sang him his favorite song, one she had learned in Girl Scouts:

> *Kookaburra sits on the old gum tree,*
> *Merry, merry king of the bush is he,*
> *Laugh! Kookaburra!*
> *Laugh! Kookaburra!*
> *Gay, your life must be!*

Jude laughed and drooled and threw his head back and blinked his eyes. He had a sweet, dimpled face like the Gerber baby and the same little swirl of brown hair on top of his head like an ice cream cone from the Dairy Queen. His skin was as soft as the quilted satin bed jacket Beryl Ann had found in the nickel bin at St. Anthony's white elephant sale. He was a beautiful, perfect baby, except for his arms. Instead of arms, Jude had two tiny appendages, one like a flipper, the other like a frog's leg. "Phocomelia" it's called, from the Greek *phokē* for "seal," and *melos* for "limb." The right one — the flipper — was just a flap of skin, void of bone, muscle, and cartilage, and was later amputated, but the left one had a three-fingered "hand" with which Jude could grasp things and shake his tiny rattle.

DR. ELSWORTH SAID that the chances were one in a billion that a thing like this could happen, and other than the deformity, the baby was healthy. The day after he was born, though, when the nurse on the afternoon shift brought Jude to Alma, she mentioned that she had seen babies born with tails and one once with gills like two little fluted tree ears on either side of the baby's neck. Only as big as this much of her thumb they were, and the pediatrician sliced them off with a scalpel and put them in a jar of formaldehyde and displayed them in a glass case in his office as if they were a delicacy, and she could never look at canned mushrooms again, she said, and to this day even the sight of sliced mushrooms on a pizza gave her the heebiejeebies. This was years ago, she said, when she was in nursing school, and just the tiniest scar was left on the baby's neck, just a pale pink scar like a neat embroidery stitch. An atavism it was called, meaning "throwback," she said. That baby was a girl.

This nurse — Willa was her name — had a friend who was a pediatric nurse in Pittsburgh, and just two weeks ago, she said, a baby with no arms had been delivered at Mercy Hospital there, and she'd heard about another birth up near Erie: same thing.

Some people in Indian Gap whispered that Jude was cursed and other things about the devil. *The sins of the father,* they said, *are visited unto the children,* they said, *into the third and fourth genera-tions* . . . and as Jude grew, the tiny arm remained a small am-phibian appendage like one of Tyrannosaurus rex's, which was the name the other children — mean as only children can be — called him. And when the children mocked him, crying out, "Hey, Tyrannosaurus! Hey, Beryl Ann, how's your little dino-saur?" Beryl Ann chased after them, and if she caught up with them, she pulled their hair and hit them with her fists and kicked them with her dirty Keds.

SOME YEARS LATER, when Beryl Ann was nineteen and missed her period and began to think she was pregnant, it was October, and she was a sophomore at the nursing school in Pitts-burgh. She didn't know what to do. She wasn't in love with the father of her baby. Marriage was out of the question — he wasn't even around. And she didn't want to disgrace her par-ents. Abortions were illegal then; still, it was common knowl-edge that one could be had in Philadelphia, D.C., New York, or even right in Pittsburgh for two thousand dollars, but where would someone like her come up with that kind of money? Abortions were for rich women.

And were they morally wrong? Some people said that the fe-tus was a perfect human being, complete with soul, at the mo-ment of conception, when it was no bigger than a dust mote, a microscopic sea monkey, a single cell. Others argued that the soul entered the body at the moment of birth, not conception, and still others took the middle road, sure that the fertilized egg wasn't human until a certain — hotly debatable — develop-mental stage. And the feminists said, no matter what, a woman had the right to control her own body.

For Beryl Ann, though, pregnancy wasn't a philosophical is-sue at all, it was an economic one. If she was pregnant, an abortion was out of the question because it cost too much, and the prohibitive cost eliminated the moral dilemma. Whatever she chose to do would be based on the reality that she was unmarried, unemployed, and living off of a Kiwanis Club scholarship and student loans.

Beryl's knees were knocking and her teeth were chattering when it was her turn to use the pay phone out in the dormitory hall. Her heart was pounding in her ears and in her chest with the racket of the Sans Souci Lanes bowling alley when she called the clinic to get the results of the pregnancy test. In her bell-bottom jeans and Navy surplus sweater, she pressed between the phone booth and the radiator, leaning her forehead against the sticky plastic sign that read PLEASE LIMIT YOUR CALLS TO THREE MINUTES, knowing the answer before the nurse even said it. That one time with Vinny was the only time she hadn't used any contraception, and wouldn't you know it, wouldn't you know she'd end up pregnant?

Vincent Devron, the father of Beryl Ann's baby, had been drafted and was in boot camp at Fort Jackson in South Carolina. Three more weeks and then Vietnam. He and Beryl were not really serious, but she had let him have her in the backseat of a Plymouth in a used car lot out on the Old Indian River Road on a hot Saturday night, the weekend before he was to report to the Cook County draft. They had been at a party over Labor Day weekend, making out and smoking grass and drinking Colt 45, and when they left, Vinny pulled the Plymouth into Wally Walker's used car lot and turned off the ignition, and Beryl got out and wrote on the windshield with lipstick $800 FIRM, and then they crawled in the backseat and did it. A "mercy fuck," her friend Gloria called it, and sometimes Beryl Ann hated the way Gloria talked.

Once the clinic confirmed what Beryl Ann already knew, it didn't take her long to make up her mind. She was not going to drop out of school and go back to Indian Creek and disgrace her parents, and she was not going to tell Vinny about any of this, and she was not going to try to raise this child by herself. She would give the baby up for adoption. She could do it. She was young and healthy, and the baby would be healthy, and there were plenty of married couples out there — good people — who wanted a baby and couldn't have one for whatever reason, and they would give this child a life of opportunity that she surely never could provide, and this would never happen again.

She thought of little Jude, who was in first grade, and how she loved him and how when he was a baby she pretended he was hers, but now, faced with the reality of single parenthood, the prospect was overwhelming. She couldn't do it.

St. Anthony's would arrange the adoption and pay the hospital bills. The baby was due in mid-April, and Beryl could hide the pregnancy through the Christmas holidays and through winter, she figured, and hopefully the baby would come early, on a weekend, maybe Easter even.

Early April and Vincent Devron was missing in action somewhere on the Mekong Delta, and Alma and Beryl's father was dying of black lung disease. His lungs were slowly hardening like plaster of Paris, as if metamorphosing into the coal he had spent so many years hacking at. Now when he inhaled there was no place for the air to go except a tiny fissure in his petrified left lung. Beryl Ann's mother called her and told her to come home, come home, her father was dying. Early April and the world was yellowing with daffodils and forsythia, and little coltsfoot in the ditches, and the beautiful yellow-green of willows, and from somewhere behind the brown hills a pink seashell nightlight seemed to be burning, but Beryl was big as a barn and ashamed and did not go. Alma called and pleaded with her sister, *Come home,* but Beryl did not want her mother and father to see her. She waited two days, not knowing what to do. Then she took the bus to Indian Creek, and as she walked up the alley she could see from the corner the cars and the people on the porch, and she knew.

Beryl's denim jacket strained around her as she stepped up on the porch and walked past the neighbors and through the door. Her mother stood up from the La-Z-Boy in her apron and pilled gray cardigan and slapped her across the face. "How could you?" she sobbed. "How could you?"

Beryl continued walking, through the dining room with its cuckoo clock and its companion prints above the buffet — Jesus on his knees, praying in the Garden of Gethsemane; Jesus knocking on someone's blue door — and through the kitchen, with its ceramic sacred heart on the wall like a big, bloodied fist, and out the back door where a mound of wet laundry sat in a wicker basket on the stoop.

Beryl leaned over as best she could and picked up the basket and carried it on her hip out to the clothesline. She hung up the laundry, shaking each piece, snapping out the wrinkles, stretching and pinning and joining everything carefully on the line, inhaling deep the sharp bleach smell of the bright white walls of sheets.

In an upstairs window, wound in a lace curtain that smelled like dust and boiled cabbage, rubbing alcohol, Jergens lotion, and death, a little boy stood in the room where his grandfather had died. The bed had been stripped, and the door was closed. A black-faced clock ticked loudly on the dresser beside a can of Lysol with a shiny gold cap. From his secret, sheer chrysalis, Jude looked down on the backyard and at his favorite aunt and wondered at how big she had grown in the belly and how her flowered dress hung high in the front and swooped down low in the back. He leaned close and tapped on the window with his little hand. "Aunt Beryl, Aunt Beryl," he called out just above a whisper, but Beryl Ann didn't hear him. She didn't look up from the panels of flapping sheets. A mockingbird landed on a silver maple branch just in front of Jude. It cocked its head and hopped and turned a bright eye on the boy in the lace cocoon, then flicked its slender tail a few times and flew off into the flat sky.

Beryl Ann finished hanging the laundry and stuck the notched pole under the line, pushing the bedclothes up until they flapped and waved like the banners advertising Wally Walker's used cars. Then she walked to the end of the clothesline, past the stack of gray tomato stakes and the pussy willow at the corner of the block garage, and stepped out into the alley. She shoved her red hands into her pockets, pressing her fingers against the strange new life kicking inside her, and disappeared behind the garage, down the alley, toward the river, the asylum, and the Indian burial mound.

The Honor of Your Presence

Maggie is pacing in my office, gnawing on a no. 2 lead pencil like it's a miniature ear of corn. She has nearly all the yellow paint and white pine chewed off on one part, right down to the lead shaft. It's a disgusting habit, if you ask me, like sucking on pennies, which she also does. I wash them, she says, but still: yuck! I've seen her eat paste and rubber cement, little wads of the *Sunday Leader,* and globs of drywall spackle. I've seen her stick her finger in a can of paint and lick it off like it was icing. What it is, is a mineral deficiency called pica, a word that comes from the Latin word for magpie, a bird known for its indiscriminate appetite. Maggie Magpie I sometimes call her.

"Can't you just see a doctor, Maggie, or take a mineral supplement?" I suggested gently once when I'd caught her surreptitiously nibbling on a piece of plaster from my cracked kitchen wall.

"It's harmless, Bobbie. Leave me alone, will ya?" she insisted.

Whatever . . . you can't tell Maggie anything. I'm one of the few people — maybe the only person alive now — who knows about Maggie and her pica disorder. Usually she hides it, indulges it in private, like grownups who suck their thumbs, or teenage girls with bulimia, or anybody with some secret, socially unacceptable vice. I don't even think her husband — I mean her ex-husband — Hunter, knew about it. Mommy knew, but Mommy's been dead now for years.

"Bonds," Maggie says, pointing her chewed-up pencil at me. The pencil looks like it's done some time in a garbage disposal. "It's got to say bonds. Bonds of marriage. Not just 'twenty-six years of marriage.' Twenty-six years of the *bonds* of marriage . . . or the bondage of marriage . . . whaddaya think, Bobbie? Marital bondage. Oh, I don't know. Just put twenty-six years of hell. Hell with a capital H.

"But it's got to say bonds somewhere," she continues before I can comment. "It's too good a word to pass on. Let me see what we have so far. Hey, Bobbie, is it bonds or bands?" she asks, squinching her eyebrows. "They posted their bands? They posted their bonds? What the hell does that mean? And connubial. What kind of word is that? Connubial or cannibal? Cannibal cannabis bliss."

Maggie leans over me, her graying light brown hair brushing my shoulder, and starts running the point of her chewed-up pencil along the text on my monitor. "And consummate!" she says. "That's another one! That's a soup, for chrissake . . . isn't it? Isn't it, Bobbie? God, I'm getting so confused!"

Maggie has another disorder, too, in addition to the pica thing. It's a mild aphasia, the result of a concussion from a car accident she and Hunter were in a long time ago, before Tess was born. It's a kind of word blindness. Maggie gets words mixed up, even more so when she's stressed out. The doctors said she'd get over it, but she never did, and she's certainly not going to now after all these years. Considering the extent of her injuries and the fact that she had amnesia that took her almost two years to recover from, the aphasia is nothing. We're all used to it, including Maggie, and you can't help but laugh at some of the blunders she makes. It's like she's got some April Fool's–edition dictionary in her head, she says.

"Meet my wife, Mrs. Malaprop," Hunter used to joke.

"What about 'plight their trough'? That's a good one, too," Maggie goes on. "Whenever I hear that I think of farm animals. Pigs. Pigs in particular. Or is it troth? I don't know. I just don't know. What do I know? Plight their trough? Plight? Or plait? How do you spell that, Bobbie?"

"Maggie," I say, moving her hand away from my computer screen, "please don't write on the monitor, OK? This isn't *Winky Dink*. Just relax. Sit down."

"Sorry," she says. "Sorry, Charlie. Only the best tuna get to be Starkist," Maggie says in a deep voice, tucking in her chin and imitating a tuna fish commercial from the sixties. In the commercial, all these big tunas are smiling and yukking it up in a net that's being reeled in by a tuna boat. This puny, homely little tuna worms his way in with the big guys in the net and is grinning ear to ear as he's pulled aboard too. A second later, he's thrown back in the water with a plop. The little homely tuna turns and looks into all the living rooms across America and cries, and a voice like Don Pardo's pronounces the little tuna's fate: "Sorry, Charlie . . ."

"Waaaa!" Maggie and I say in unison, speaking for the rejected tuna.

"Wait. I'll just print it. I'll print two copies, and then we'll both just sit here and look at it and revise it together," I say. I'm trying to calm her down. I send the invitation to print, and Maggie produces a pack of Merit Ultra Lights 100s from her purse and lights up a cigarette with a shiny Zippo lighter. I recognize the lighter as the one engraved with Hunter's initials, the one

Maggie gave him as a graduation present back in the good ol' days, when everybody smoked and an engraved cigarette lighter was considered a perfectly acceptable, classy gift.

"Maggie!" I say, puzzled, "when did you start smoking again?" (I love the smell of butane and the glorious little blue flame, the lighter fluid in its flimsy can with the tiny yellow-capped tip, the flint, the click of the lighter, the friction of thumb against wheel: the ritual of smoking.)

"You're not supposed to smoke in here. It's a smoke-free workplace," I tell her.

Maggie kicks my office door shut. "This very second," she says. "I started smoking again this very second," and I don't comment. I'm tempted myself even though it's been what, six, seven years since I last lit up?

"Here, use this," I say, dumping the paper clips out of their ceramic holder and handing it to her, but Maggie isn't listening. She takes a long drag, coughs, studies the two Lassie paint-by-number paintings above my desk — one done by me, one done by her when we were kids — then flicks an ash onto the carpet, grinds it into the tweed nap with the toe of her shoe. I take a deep breath. The smoke smells good.

"You really fucked up the nose on yours," Maggie says, coughing again, pointing with her cigarette to the Lassie profile on the right.

"I was nine years old," I say defensively, "and if you'll recall," I tease, "Miss Georgia O'Keeffe, Miss Mary Cassatt, I believe you did *Jesus in the Garden of Gethsemane* right after you finished your Lassie, and Jesus looked like a damn werewolf. And you had two years on me!"

"Shut up, Bobbie!" Maggie jokes and pinches my upper arm, and I reach out to pinch her back, but Maggie's too quick. I close my eyes and savor the cigarette smoke. Behind my eyelids I see a sheet of blue, then silver, and then the tinfoil-covered cookie sheet full of miniature paint-by-number bottles with their white stenciled numbers: 4, 8, 37, 18, 22; Maggie and I in the kitchen with our new easels and "smocks" — two of Daddy's old dress shirts with the arms cut off. The painstaking toil, the great na-ive intent, the hideous results, the disappointment — no matter how far back you stood or how much you squinted — of paint-by-numbers.

My reverie is interrupted by the intercom's buzz. It's Jack, my friend and confidant in the office next to mine. "You rang?" I say flatly into the receiver, speaking like Jeeves the Butler.

"Surely we're not smoking over there, are we now?" Jack says in his *Mommie Dearest* voice.

"It's not me. It's Maggie. She just stopped by. I'm doing the invitation."

"Tell her it will kill her," he says, and hangs up, but a second later he calls back.

"I've reported this infraction to Occupational Safety and Health, and I'm suing you and your sister for exposing me to secondhand smoke," he adds in an authoritative voice at least an octave lower than his normal speaking voice. In the background I hear a snippet of Bob Dylan singing "Ballad of a Thin Man," and Jack hangs up.

Jack is one of my best friends. We hit it off from the week he started working here at Optimum Advertising five years ago, when he turned to me at his first staff meeting and whispered, "Who's the dude with the teeth?"

It was the president.

But it was my paint-by-number Lassie that won him over. Jack's partner, Lew, who died two years ago, was an antique/ junk dealer, a flea market hound, a paint-by-numbers aficio-nado. Talk about a crackpot. He and Jack collected paint-by-numbers — but not just any old paint-by-numbers. Paint-by-numbers of da Vinci's *The Last Supper* exclusively. Last count,

Jack had one hundred thirty-seven paint-by-numbers of *The Last Supper,* all in various stages of completion, all framed and hanging everywhere in his house and garage. There's even one on the front porch and one in the basement above the washer and dryer, one behind Plexiglas inside the guest bathroom shower stall. Before I knew it, I was spending every single Saturday with Lew and Jack, haunting flea markets and antique stores, estate sales, yard sales, garage sales, tag sales: a never-ending quest for paint-by-numbers of *The Last Supper.*

We were all so taken by one paint-by-number of *The Last Supper* that Jack and I were inspired to develop (on Optimum time, of course) a complete line of products and an ad campaign for a phantom company we named Christian Consumers, which we surreptitiously refer to as CC and work on constantly (on Optimum time, of course). CC's line of products includes Meals for Christians on the Go, called — guess what? — the Last Suppers. Last Suppers are microwavable meals, all displaying da Vinci's *The Last Supper* on the carton and offering Italian (spaghetti and meatballs), Mexican (chiles rellenos), American (mac and cheese, fish sticks, and meatloaf), Southern (fried chicken), Chinese (chop suey), and Middle Eastern entrees (falafel, gyros, and tabouleh), with photos of these tasty dishes cut and pasted onto that big banquet table everybody for some weird reason chose to sit on just one side of.

There's also a line of right-wing Christian video games designed as companions to the Left Behind books. Games like Queers & Christians, Armageddon or Bust, and Rapture! Rapture! challenge players age seven to adult to stalk patrons of gay bookstores, liberal politicians, abortion clinic staff, Planned Parenthood advocates, and the like during the dark and chaotic seven-year apocalyptic battle between good and evil. "Christian" players rack up points by capturing and disemboweling their heathen foe.

CC recently entered the automobile industry with hybrid vehicles: the Annunciation, the Assumption, the Trinity, the Disciple, the Wedding Guest, and the Sermon on the Mount. (We add a new one every week.) There's a luxury car, the Passion, a little scooter called the Icon, a monster truck, the Stigmata, a compact called the Miracle, and an SUV we named the IHS (although we haven't figured out yet what that stands for). Ad campaigns depict Jesus turning a jug of water into a barrel of crude oil and Jesus fueling the masses: converting a gallon of gasoline into enough alternative fuel to fill the tanks of every vehicle — Vespas to Hummers to tour buses — parked in the Mount parking lot.

Jack, CEO and marketing and artistic director of CC, has offered (read: jumped at the chance) to host the divorce party Maggie is planning. He loves parties — the organizing, the decorating, the menu planning, the cut flower arranging — the stuff Maggie and I hate. Maggie's got the money, and Jack's hot to spend it. Plus, like a true collector, he loves showing off his *Last Supper* collection. He loves Martha Stewart, too, and subscribes to her magazine. He reads all the dirt about her in the grocery store tabloids.

"That bitch Martha," Jack says, "I *love* her! I wanna have her babies."

"Gawd, am i dizzy!" Maggie says and plops down in my side chair. "Why did you let me smoke that cigarette, Bobbie? I don't feel so good. Waaaa! Whadda we got?" Maggie asks.

I hand her a copy of the invitation. She leans back in the chair and bangs her head on the wall. She bangs it again — and again, intentionally — and I reach for a red pen and start to read:

Margaret Jean Flannery requests the honor of your presence
at a celebration commemorating the dissolution of twenty-
six years of the bonds of marriage between herself and J.

Hunter Stone on the thirtieth day of May in the 2000th year
of our Lord —

"Two thousandth?" Maggie interrupts. "How do you say
that? That sounds funny. Two thousandth?" she says again,
then adds a little bar of "All I Want for Christmas Is My Two
Front Teeth": "Thithter thuthie thittin' on a thithle," she sings.

AFTER AT LEAST a dozen more revisions, we finally get the
text just right, and I fix the whole thing up the way Maggie
wants it, like a negative of a real wedding invitation, with Shel-
ley Allegro — a fancy serif font — in white on a black background, with white wedding bells. I check that my boss is still
out and send one hundred of the invitations to print on specialty
paper I ordered from Paper Direct on our company account. I
lean in Jack's doorway, keeping one eye on the printer, the other
on the door to our office suite. These damn black invitations are
going to use up the entire toner cartridge, I'm sure. Oh well,
what the hell? I figure I'm underpaid, and the benefits suck; Optimum owes me enough to underwrite my sister's divorce party
invitations.

Maggie is now in Jack's office, studying her reflection in the
glass of his framed Pratt Institute diploma, putting on orange
lipstick. "Tangerine Fizz," she says, smiling like Lucille Ball.
"Like it?"

"I have a great idea for the cake," Jack announces. He's supposed to be working on a Blimpie's ad campaign, but I can see
he's been bidding on stuff on eBay, probably paint-by-numbers.
Why else would he have an egg timer by his keyboard? He leans
back and rubs his head. He's bald or nearly so. Has his head
shaved, "smooth as a you-know-what," he says. His eyebrows
are pale, and his eyes are very blue.

"You won't believe it. It's so brilliant. Einstein couldn't have
come up with a better cake. Nor Betty Crocker. Nor Julia. Nor

even Martha! Listen," Jack goes on. "Bittersweet," he whispers, leaning across his desk. "Hardly any sugar. Just enough to make it edible. A teaspoon. Very bitter. And *black*."

Maggie is making smacking sounds with her tangerine-fizzed lips.

"Chocolate so dark it's almost black. And add a whole bottle each of red and blue food coloring. That will blacken it up real good. Deep, rich undertones. *Very* symbolic." He pauses. "Now here's the best part: *tiered*." He enunciates the word like he's the emcee at a spelling bee. "Just like a wedding cake, right? But get this . . ." He pauses dramatically again and leans forward. "*Leaning*," he says slowly. "*Askew*," he says even more slowly, drawing out both syllables.

"Leaning like the Leaning Tower of Pizza!" Maggie pipes up.

"Pisa," I correct.

"And on the top, we'll get one of those cake toppers and I'll get a hacksaw and I'll hack off the groom and then I'll paint the bride's dress black . . ." Jack has jumped up and is talking a mile a minute. He and Maggie have this way of getting each other going, of feeding off each other like symbiotic fungi.

"And big, too. I want a *big* cake. Bigger than my wedding cake." Maggie jumps up, too. "I want a cake as big as the cake Elizabeth Taylor cut to celebrate the opening of *Around the World in Eighty Days*. I saw this movie clip of her cutting it on *Tribute*."

"I saw her cut it on live TV when I was in fifth grade," Jack says. "I *love* Elizabeth Taylor," he adds. "I *loved National Velvet*, oh, and *Cat on a Hot Tin Roof*. But of course, by that time I was in love with Paul Newman. Oh, god, he was so bee-u-tee-ful in that."

"They had this staircase on wheels," Maggie continues. "It was curved and magnificent — like out of *Gone with the Wind*

— and they wheeled it over to this cake that was the size of the Lincoln Memorial, and Elizabeth Taylor came out in this white chiffon dress, all sparkly and flowing —"

"I *loved* that dress!" Jack gasps. "It was a Schiaparelli! It was so *gorgeous!*"

"— and walked up the staircase and cut a little slice of cake off the top layer, and there was a great applause and thousands of balloons were —"

"Where was this?" I interrupt, only half listening.

"I don't know *where!* It was on TV. In Hollywood, probably," Maggie says. "I don't know where it was. Who cares where it was, for god's sake? You ask the dumbest questions, Bobbie."

"A few weeks later he died in a plane crash," Jack says.

"Who?" I ask. "Who died in a plane crash?"

"Mike Todd. You know, her husband. Elizabeth Taylor's husband, the guy who made the movie," Jack says.

"What movie? I thought she was married to Eddie Fisher, Carrie Fisher's father." I'm totally lost. It's tough watching the printer and the door at the same time.

"*Around the World in Eighty Days.* You know, Jules Verne," Maggie adds.

"He was murdered. A bomb in his private plane," Jack goes on.

"Jules Verne?" Maggie says. "Murdered?"

"No! Mike Todd!" Jack says.

"Murdered? You're kidding. I never heard that," I say.

"Me neither," says Maggie.

"Oh, yeah, it was all McCarthy era stuff. J. Edgar Hoover had him killed. Mike Todd worked for the FBI, but he was really a double agent, working for the Soviet Union. He was a Russian spy!"

"You're kidding. Elizabeth Taylor was married to a Russian spy? Where did you hear that?"

"Oh, you know . . . around," Jack says. "Elizabeth Taylor didn't know it, but Mike Todd definitely was a Russian spy, and he was murdered all right. Every now and then his picture shows up in the *National Enquirer* along with Marilyn Monroe, Elvis, JFK, Lady Di —"

"Martha Stewart," I add.

"Thank you!" Jack says in a curt, nasal voice. "You know, it's out there. It's common knowledge. They were all murdered. Every single one of them. Jesus," he says, "where have you girls been all your lives?"

"I don't know," I say. And I mean it.

Maggie doesn't reply.

"Maybe Martha Stewart is next," I add just to be smart. "Maybe she's a Russian spy, too. Ever think of that?"

Now it's midnight, Saturday night, a week before Maggie's divorce party, and Maggie is dyeing her wedding dress at Miller's Wash House on Eighth Street. She's dragged me along. absolutely no dying three big signs warn, and I have to laugh because dyeing is spelled wrong, and the thought of somebody intentionally crawling in here — of all places — to die just cracks me up.

"Cover me," Maggie says as she opens the Wal-Mart bag and pulls out a dozen bottles of Ritz black dye, lining them up on the folding table, tearing off the aluminum foil seals with her teeth. I see her lick one seal before tossing it in the garbage; I don't say anything, but her tongue looks like a chow's. She's stuffed her wedding gown, train and all, into one of those big five-dollar front-loaders.

"I can't believe I'm letting you do this," I say.

"I can't believe I'm letting myself do this."

There's no way Maggie could ever squeeze into this size-seven gown, but not to worry. She has this plan of slitting the side seams open and lacing the dress back together with black leather cord. "The Black Heidi," Jack has already named the gown. She'll do it, too. Nothing will stop her. She's so angry with Hunter. *Closure,* she says. She just wants some *closure.* Not revenge, *closure.* And she wants it all out in the open and over with. She says she's not going to be running into people at Giant Eagle a year from now and have them say, *Oh, Maggie, Maggie, how are you?* and *How's Hunter?* and *How's Tess doing in school?* No. She wants it out in the open. Her first idea was to publish an announcement in the *Leader,* telling it like it is, how Hunter was leaving her for one of his junior partners, Melanie Nevarro, how they'd been carrying on behind her back for years.

"Libel," Jack pointed out. "That's with a capital *L*, capital *I*, capital *B* . . ."

I think Maggie could have handled the divorce business. It was the annulment that got her goat. She's not even Catholic and neither is Hunter. The whole thing is just absurd.

"Damnit all anyway," Maggie says. "*We were married!* Grant me that, we were married. No way in hell am I going to agree to something that says we were never married. God can send a lightning bolt and strike me dead, but no guy in a big stupid mitre box is going to say Hunter and I were never married. We were married. We had witnesses for chrissake. The church was full of people. We were married for twenty-six goddamn years! And if we weren't married, just what does that make Tess? Tell me that. What does that make Tess if Hunter and I were never married? *We were friggin' married.*"

Tess is Maggie and Hunter's only child. She just turned nineteen in March. She has blue hair about a half-inch long, a pierced nostril and a pierced lip, pierced ears and a pierced tongue — and that's only the parts you can see.

"It's a formality, a legal formality," Hunter argued in his lawyer voice. "Melanie is Catholic. It would make a difference to her." He had the balls to say that: It would make a difference to Melanie.

"Fuck formality," Maggie said. "I don't care if Melanie Nevarro is really the Virgin Frigate Mary in a van Claiborne suit, this marriage is not being annulled," and she threw a Tupperware container of gazpacho at him. Maggie has never been one to swear — or throw things, for that matter — but ever since this annulment business, every other word is a four-letter one, but I'd rather that than tears. She's angry. She shows it. She says if anybody would have seen Hunter in his Brooks Brothers suit splattered with gazpacho they would have called nine-friggin'-one-one.

"You know what annulment is?" Jack says. "I'll tell you what it is. Annulment is just another money-making scheme of the Catholic Church. It's for the rich and famous. Annulment is a privileged thing. It's like the Lexus of divorce. It costs at least twenty thousand dollars to get your marriage annulled. The more you've got, the more it costs."

"That's right!" Maggie chimes in. "One of the Kennedys started it. Joe Kennedy, Jr., I think."

"Yeah," Jack goes on, "he got an annulment for some outrageous amount so he could marry some skirt in his office. But his ex-wife, now she didn't take it sitting down. No sirree! She wrote a book about it and smeared his name but good. I mean a *royal* smear. It was just like Henry VIII and Anne Boleyn all over again."

"Wasn't she beheaded?" Maggie asks.

IF I WANTED to dwell on it, I would wonder if Maggie really kept the wedding vows she's now so crazy about defending. There was a time years back when I could have sworn Maggie had a thing going on with Graham Buchannan. I mean if I were on a witness stand I couldn't say for sure, but there was this one time at a barbecue at Maggie and Hunter's when I walked into the kitchen and Graham and Maggie were together, and there was this awkwardness, this terrible awkwardness when I walked in, as if some forbidden words or some illicit gesture had just passed between them, and well, sometimes that's all it takes to know. I never forgot it. And Graham had a reputation for being a ladies' man. I don't know how Celeste put up with him all those years. In my mind, I've rehearsed that moment in the kitchen a thousand times, but I wasn't about to pry. *Live and let live,* I always say. *Live and let live,* it's good advice. *There but for the grace of God,* our Grandmother Flannery always said.

Sometimes I think that really the only good advice is found in clichés and aphorisms. Like it's all been said before and all our human experiences are just age-old repetitions, the same balderdash, just condensed, distilled, refined, reduced to a handful of trite sayings: *There is nothing new under the sun. Live and let live. People who live in glass houses . . .* that kind of thing. Maggie is not unreasonable, just high strung. She'll deal with this divorce. I know she will. *Take a Valium like a normal person,* we say to each other. It's a line from the movie *Desperately Seeking Susan.* It means cope, damnit. Cope. Maggie knows how. We both do.

I'M STANDING LOOKOUT, still watching the laudromat parking lot for the owner, Mr. Miller. Maggie is smoking, eating a peppermint patty she just got out of the snack machine, and watching her wedding dress turn black and churn. She says she'll smoke her last cigarette at the party.

"For years," Maggie says, peering into the washer as if it were a deep-sea aquarium at SeaWorld, "I thought Tess would wear that dress. I was saving it for her. Shit. Now look at it. It cost three hundred dollars back in 1974. That was a fortune then, but Mommy wanted me to have the one I wanted. That was probably more money than Daddy made in a week. And we thought it would be a keepsake, an heirloom. Someday my daughter will wear it, I thought." She says all this, and I can hear in her voice that she might start crying.

"She still might," I say. "Tess still might wear it after all. Just wait and see, Maggie. Just you wait and see," I say as a dark convertible with fins pulls into Miller's Wash House parking lot.

THE INVITATIONS HAVE gone out, and all the RSVPs have come back like boomerangs. It's the night of the divorce party and no one wants to miss this event. "Mom, you've got moxie," Tess says, lacing up Maggie's dress. Maggie is getting more and more nervous. She's even sent an invitation to Hunter and Melanie Nevarro. Surely neither of them would dare make an appearance tonight. Would they? Could she have done it just out of spite? *Closure,* she keeps saying, not spite. *Closure.* Where did she get that word?

Jack is in his element. His lovely little lake house is on display, decorated to the hilt. Black crepe paper streamers, black and purple balloons, bows, tea lights, gladiola, roses, calla lilies. One hundred thirty-seven Jesuses. One thousand six hundred forty-four disciples. Jack is wearing black Calvin Klein jeans, a black Calvin Klein T-shirt, a vintage white tuxedo jacket, an orchid boutonniere, one diamond stud earring, and a small black button that says DENIAL PLUS PROZAC. IT WORKS FOR ME.

I'm wearing my vintage tux, too. A black cutaway with tails, starched white bib, and black satin cummerbund. Jack found it for me at Goodwill. Like new. I was in housewares and he came running up with it. "Cart!" he hollered. "Cart!" It's this code we have for what we'll have in our shopping carts when we're out on the street like two old bag ladies — after we've been fired from Optimum for goofing off, and we've let everything go. "Cart" means "this is priceless, this is something you must keep forever." It's the highest distinction that can be bestowed upon any garment, any accessory, any thing. And Jack was right. The tux fits me to a tee and looks great with red Chuck Taylor hightops.

I'm still sick though about Maggie's dress when I think about her wedding. The photograph of her sitting at the vanity in our bedroom on Cher-Lee Circle, putting on her headpiece and veil. And Mommy in her blue lace mother-of-the-bride dress, Daddy looking dapper in a tux, but underneath his lungs half gone. Twenty-six years turning into this one crazy night. But I have to admit that dress looks damn good for what it's been through at Miller's, and Maggie looks like a million dollars. Tess has highlighted Maggie's hair, and Maggie's lost a bit of weight. The annulment diet, she calls it.

Tess has put grommets up the sides of the gown and done a beautiful job on the leather lacing. She's fashioned a divorce bouquet out of tinfoil and colored cellophane "roses" and Fourth of July sparklers — of all things. O.B. tampons spray-painted Day-Glo green dangle from their strings down the front of the bouquet, imitating some kind of greenery. I imagine Tess intends to light this contraption at some point, rather than throw it, but who knows? Maggie has prepared a speech, but she won't let me hear it or see it. She's got it rolled up like a scroll and tied with a black satin ribbon. It's about closure is all she'll say.

The party's in full swing. Jack has made all kinds of hors d'oeuvres. Minted meatballs, basiled goat cheese, mango and cilantro salsa, California rolls, and so many desserts I can't even keep them straight. He's even rented a chocolate fountain. Joni Mitchell is singing. Brother Bob and Joni are Jack's favorites. Now it's "Sharon's Song," one of my absolute favorites.

There's even a table full of gifts. And the cake, the cake is spectacular. Jack had a professional baker make it to his specifications. It's definitely black. Black as shoe polish and with a gravity-defying tilt. And big. Not anywhere near as big as Elizabeth Taylor's of course, but pretty damn big. Each tier is supported by six-inch pillars spray-painted black, and the cake stands a good three feet above the table, towering over everything, and leaning. *Leaning.*

WE'RE UPSTAIRS IN Jack's bedroom — Maggie and Tess and me — freshening up, and Maggie's getting cold feet. She's had too much to drink and her face is flushed. I've had one glass of Rioja too many, and I was so nervous, I went out and bought a box of Nicorette gum a few days ago and have chewed almost the whole thing. My head is winking.

"Mom, your arms look horrible in a sleeveless dress," Tess announces. "You should have worn a sweater or a shawl, I'm telling you. Your arms look like legs."

"What your friends won't tell you . . . ," Maggie says, rolling her eyes.

"Speech! Speech!" we hear Jack calling from downstairs.

"Waaaaa!" Maggie and I say.

Tess joins in the tuna chorus. "Waaaaa!"

"Shit," Maggie says. "How did this happen? How did my life turn into the opposite, the negative of what I thought it would be? What have I become? What if Mommy and Daddy were alive? What would they think of me?"

"Remember what Grandma Flannery used to say when we cried?" I remind her.

"Save your tears. You'll need them when you grow up."

"Yeah. Did you save any, Maggie Magpie?"

"Nope. Not a one," Maggie says.

"Me neither," I say. "Let's go. Let's hit it. Let's get this damn closure thing over with."

"Here comes the divorcée," Jack is singing, "all step aside," as Maggie and Tess and I descend the stairs. Tess is holding Maggie's train. "She is so bee-u-tee-ful, here she comes . . ."

There's a great commotion, then everyone grows quiet.

Maggie's standing with Tess now at the far end of the living room, against the fireplace, holding a glass of champagne and her rolled-up speech. Tess is wearing what looks like a purple slip under a black leather motorcycle jacket. She's got on fishnet stockings and black combat boots and a reflective green rhinestone-studded dog collar. Behind them hangs the crown jewel *Last Supper.* It was Lew's pride and joy. Bought in a yard sale just a few miles from here, down Little Indian Creek Road, right before the interstate overpass.

"We were driving along about fifty miles an hour, and there it was," Lew used to tell. "There it was leaning against one of those Sears faux-walnut-case dehumidifiers, an avocado green crockpot propped in front to keep it from blowing over."

"He spotted it at fifty miles per hour," Jack would pick up the story. "'Stop,' Lew yelled, and I almost ran off the road. 'I see one!' Lew hollered. He ran up the driveway like his pants were on fire." Jack would laugh hysterically telling it.

They had it framed professionally in a gaudy, gilded frame fit for a Titian and hung it above the mantle. It's about a three-quarters complete paint-by-number of da Vinci's *The Last Supper.* And then some. Very realistic-looking Chinese carry-out containers are strewn across the table, and a Domino's pizza box supports some disciple's bare feet. Peter, is it? Paul? Judas Escargo (as Maggie would say)?

"These two old people had it," Jack said. "Said they found it in their basement, behind the furnace, but I think the old lady did it herself."

On the mantle underneath *The Last Supper* is a framed photograph of Jack and Lew standing in the same place as Maggie and Tess. It's a postmodern moment, as Jack would say, or maybe it's more like just a pound of Land O'Lakes butter.

"Once upon a time," Maggie says. She takes a deep, choppy breath, pulls in her stomach, smoothing the black satin of her gown, sets her glass on the piano, and takes Tess's hand. "All I wanted was to be Mrs. Hunter Stone."

This is not the speech she's prepared, I'm sure. She's clenching the scroll in her right hand. She lets it drop, then takes a big gulp of champagne. "I wrote that name a thousand times, ten thousand times. I wrote that name a million times: MRS. HUNTER STONE. MRS. MAGGIE STONE. MR. AND MRS. HUNTER STONE. I wrote it on fine-lined notebook paper. I wrote it on graph paper. I wrote it on steamed-up shower doors. I wrote it on the side of school buses and the hoods of dirty cars. I wrote it on my book covers. I wrote it in the frost. I wrote it in the snow. I wrote it in the sky with my index finger, and I traced the letters on my skirt under my desk in every class, and I wrote it on my pillow, my finger always moving: MRS. HUNTER STONE. MRS. HUNTER STONE. MAGGIE STONE. I wrote it on my sister's back in bed at night. Ask her. Ask Bobbie."

She says this, and I start to cry. I can't help it. I remember her doing that. I remember sleeping with her every night in the same old iron bed. I remember the chenille bedspread and the faded blue satin bed skirt, and I remember the name I wrote, too. Lee. The name of my first lover, Lee Rollins. Just thinking of him makes my heart ache, like thinking of the dead.

"Once I wrote it with ketchup on a sidewalk. I carved it in a picnic table with Hunter's Swiss army knife," Maggie continues. "MRS. HUNTER STONE. I wrote it with Morton salt. MRS. HUNTER STONE. MAGGIE STONE. We wrote it in the sand in big tall letters at Wildwood, the day after graduation. Big letters decorated with seashells. MR. AND MRS. HUNTER STONE, we wrote together, on our hands and knees, digging out the sand with our hands, building the letters with our hands, big enough for a plane to see. Like we were shipwrecked, macarooned on a dessert island."

Maggie takes a sip and hands the champagne glass to Tess, who finishes it off. "That's all," Maggie says. "That's all. Thank you, everybody. Thank you, everyone, for being my friend. That's all. The end. Finesse."

"Finis," I say to myself.

Tess sets the champagne glass on the brick hearth, then smashes it with one hearty stomp of her steel-toed Doc Martens and gives her mother a peck on the cheek.

Applause.

A delayed whoop.

A piercing, two-finger whistle.

Somehow I suddenly feel exhausted and exhilarated, relieved, happy, and sad all at the same time. I don't know what I feel. Hell, maybe it's closure I feel! For some reason I start to think of the strangest things. I remember when Maggie and I were kids how we used to run to this Endicott & Johnson shoestore uptown, about three blocks away from our house, and stick our feet in this machine that let you see how your shoes fit. It was really an x-ray machine. You'd stand on a platform with your feet in this metal box and push this big red button. You'd look down into a little glass window on top, and for a second or two you could see all the bones in your feet, all bright white like a skeleton. We'd each do it. We'd wiggle our toes and scream and then run out. That machine wasn't around long, but it sure was fun.

The other thing we used to do was stand in the bathroom doorway and press the insides of our wrists against the jamb while we counted to sixty. When you stepped away from the doorway, your arms just rose up involuntarily as if you were about to fly. "Angel" we called that game.

I don't know why I'm remembering these things. I just am.

"Dance with me, OK?" Maggie insists, taking my hand. "Dance with me like we used to dance when we were just two silly girls pretending we were dancing with boys. Before there were any boys. Before there were boys or men to break our hearts. When there were just girls. Come on, honey," she says to Tess, "dance with your old, crazy, divorced mom — your crazy, old, annealed mum — and her crazy, divorced sister."

But Tess declines. "Uhm, I don't think so," she says almost

shyly, "but don't let me stop you," she adds, leaning back and holding up her hand like a traffic cop.

Maggie motions to Jack. He aims the remote control at the CD player and hits play. Maggie puts her left hand on my right shoulder, and I put my left hand on her right hip. Her breath smells suspiciously like Vicks VapoRub.

It ain't no use to sit and wonder why, babe

Brother Bob sings,

> *It don't matter, anyhow*
> *An' it ain't no use to sit and wonder why, babe*
> *If you don't know by now . . .*

It's not really dance music but we dance anyway, sort of gliding and box-stepping around the room in giant steps and singing along. Other couples are dancing, too: women with women, women with men, men with men, singing loudly with exaggerated Dylan inflection. Portia, my old German shorthaired pointer, crawls out from under the buffet table and dances, too, barking happily and jumping up and down around Maggie and me. Tess and Jack are doing some kind of crazy tango across the dining room and living room, also in giant steps.

"When your rooster crows at the break of dawn —" Maggie and I sing to them as they pass by cheek to cheek.

"— Look out your window and I'll be gone," they turn their Siamese twinhead and sing to us. The light is just right, and for a split second the stud in Tess's tongue flashes. Candles flicker, and across the long row of living room windows, our reflections dance, then disappear into the dark, polished woodwork.

The Wonders of the World

REGGIE DIDN'T FEEL GOOD, but he didn't say anything about it. While Florence was setting the table, Reggie rummaged through the string and tape, the batteries and rubber bands, in the kitchen junk drawer, looking for the little flashlight, and when he found it, he stuck it in his trouser pocket.

"Bring five napkins," Florence called from the dining room. "The white ones with the poinsettias . . . From the drawer underneath the microwave," she added a second later, but Reggie pretended not to hear her. He stepped into the powder room under the back stairs and quietly pulled the door shut.

The powder room — what his mother had always called it — had been Reggie's favorite room in the house ever since he was a little boy. It had once been a pantry under the back stairway, but during the early nineteen-thirties, Reggie's father and his father's brother, Uncle Stanley, converted the pantry into a much-needed bathroom. There were seven of them living there then: Reggie and his parents and his three siblings, and Reggie's grandfather, whom everyone called Angry Jack. Angry Jack had come from the old country and spoke only Gaelic. He was an old man with big, knotted brown hands like tree burls. He slept on a day bed in the sun parlor and walked with a shillelagh — a twisted black walking stick with thorns jutting from its length and a tarnished brass ferrule. Frightful as it was to Reggie when he was a boy, the shillelagh now hung in a place of honor above the mantel, underneath two old pictures — one a photograph of Angry Jack as a young man in Belfast in an Orangemen's parade, all the men carrying shillelaghs, the other a framed newspaper clipping from August 22, 1911, about Rosie Hackett and the Jacob's Biscuit Factory labor wars in Dublin.

The powder room still had the bright blue linoleum and the same wallpaper with stylized black line drawings of the Seven Wonders of the World. The linoleum and the wallpaper were remnants from the renovation of the old Sterling Hotel, a job that Reggie's father and Uncle Stanley had helped complete. The wallpaper was from the hotel lobby and the linoleum from the kitchen, which Reggie's father said was so big you could skate in it. There was a tiny white sink in the powder room, no bigger than the bowl of a drinking fountain, a white commode with a black wooden handle, a medicine cabinet above the sink, and next to the cabinet a little frosted window like a porthole that pushed out. That was all there was room for.

It had been a real engineering feat — the eighth wonder of the world, Reggie's father always joked — to squeeze all Seven Wonders of the World into the powder room, and it became a family euphemism to say you were going to visit Zeus at Olympia when you were going to the bathroom, and a favorite family prank to offer to show company the eighth wonder of the world underneath the back stairs.

WHEN HE WAS in sixth grade, Reggie was the only student in his class at St. Anthony the Abbot Catholic School for Boys and Girls who could name the Seven Wonders of the World, and his teacher was astounded. Reggie, who never attempted to answer a question unless called upon, had volunteered really without thinking when Sister Annuncianata asked if anyone could name the Seven Wonders of the World. Reggie's hand shot straight up like the hand of a mechanical toy soldier, and everyone turned around when Sister called on him.

"Yes, Reggie," Sister Annuncianata said slowly, amazed by Reggie's sudden participation, "did you hear the question?"

Reggie rose from his seat and stood beside his chair like you were supposed to do when answering a question. He closed his eyes and called up the powder room with its tiny labeled drawings: the Hanging Gardens of Babylon above the toilet; the Great Pyramid of Giza, the statue of Zeus at Olympia, and the temple of Artemis at Ephesus on the slanted ceiling; the mausoleum at Halicarnassus and the Colossus of Rhodes above the toilet paper holder; and the lighthouse of Alexandria in the slim wall space next to the medicine cabinet.

When Reggie recited the list of the Seven Wonders of the World, he mispronounced a few words: "Baby Lawn" for Babylon, he had said, and "Our Tea Miss" for Artemis, and "Eppie Hissus" for Ephesus — but Sister Annuncianata was still impressed. Her jaw dropped and she clapped the nun applause: slapping a ruler held in one hand against the palm of the other.

"Why, Reggie," she said, smiling and twisting her big crucifix, "Reggie Hackett, where did *you* learn that?"

"A . . . a . . . a book," Reggie stammered. Suddenly Reggie began to feel sick and nervous, thinking Sister Annuncianata would ask what book. But she didn't.

"That's wonderful, Reggie," she said, and right then and there, Reggie was allowed to pick up his books and his lunch pail and move to the front of his row, usurping the seat of one of the brightest students, Eunice Jeffries. With great commotion, everyone moved back one seat, but in a few days, Reggie was back in his familiar seat in the crowded room, back where he could once again lean his head against the blackboard's familiar chalk tray.

Reggie never forgot, though, sitting in the front of the room with its big windows and the wide bolts of sunlight full of dancing dust fairies pouring onto the waxed floor and shining on Sister Annuncianata's polished black shoes, their toe-tips pricked with tiny pinholes like graham crackers. In the front of the room, where the door was ajar, you could see out into the hallway, with its hotdog-colored linoleum and pale green walls. In the front of the room, you could see the ring on President Roosevelt's finger, and the colored maps that pulled up and down like huge blinds above the chalkboard.

IN THE EARLY seventies, when Reggie's own children — Albert and Faye — were in college, Albert had argued during dinner one Thanksgiving that the wonders in the powder room were not really the Seven Wonders of the World, only the seven architectural wonders of the ancient world, since the list had been compiled around the second century B.C., and that the wonders of the modern world were not architectural at all but scientific, technological, and ideological. They included, he insisted, television, satellites, and antibiotics; social and economic theories; and the invention of the binary number system, computers, and guided missiles. Faye, who was a freshman — two years behind Albert — argued that there was no comparison, that art was timeless, and that the wonders of the ancient world were every bit as astounding today as they were then.

"Fuck your guided missiles," Faye said at the dinner table, ready herself to explode.

Florence kept her head down and, half rising, offered, "More turkey, anyone? Stuffing?"

Reggie sat at the head of the table, feeling tired and old, and said nothing. He pretended to scratch behind his ear and inconspicuously turned off his hearing aid, as he often did, then busied himself with passing the serving bowls, urging, like Florence, second helpings. Mashed potatoes, creamed onions, sweet potatoes with pineapple chunks and miniature marshmallows.

When they were little, Albert and Faye were inseparable, but it seemed that as soon as they reached adolescence, they were poised like the black and white Scotty dog magnets they had once loved to play with, only now they were turned always so as to repel each other. At the time of that Thanksgiving dinner, Albert was studying prelaw. He was precise, methodical, and conservative. A young Republican. Faye had not yet chosen a major; she was a free spirit, the artsy, political, bohemian type, a champion of the underdog since she was a child. Investigations a year later revealed that she was a member of the Socialist Workers Party of America and an officer in the Students for Democratic Society, and that she belonged to any number of leftist political organizations. She wrote scathing columns in an underground newspaper, Reggie and Florence later learned, articles about the corruption of the U.S. government by big corporations. In these articles, Faye called the corporate leaders pigs and urged the poor and oppressed to stand up and fight for their inalienable rights, and for young men to burn their draft cards and flee to Canada to avoid induction.

The only time Reggie was ever in Faye's dormitory room was a few days before the Thanksgiving dinner when she and Albert had argued so. At her dorm room door, Reggie was greeted by a poster with a peace sign made of flowers and the words MAKE LOVE NOT WAR in wavy pink letters. Directly inside, a poster of a woman wearing a bandana and displaying her biceps proclaimed, WE CAN DO IT! Above Faye's bed was another poster with a portrait of a man Reggie recognized as the Argentine revolutionary Che Guevara, wearing a beret and bandolier. At the end of her freshman year, Faye would drop out of school, move to New York City, and within six months be killed.

The day Reggie and Florence got the phone call was a

Sunday, and they were just heading out the door for Mass. Florence was putting on her hat in front of the hall mirror. Reggie was getting their coats. Florence answered the phone.

"Yes," she said, "yes," in a strange, frightened voice Reggie had never heard in their twenty-five years of marriage. Reggie was frozen mid-action, his hands on the shoulders of a soft coat on a wooden hanger. The hall clock began to tick loudly, and Reggie's heart thumped in his chest, his throat, his ears, as if he were under water. His hands began to tremble, and the hangers in the coat closet rattled.

"Not our Faye," Florence said, holding on to the newel post with one hand and speaking weakly into the receiver. "Not our Faye. There must be some mistake. Dear God, please not our Faye."

A gas leak in a tenement building. An explosion. Faye and two others blown to pieces. Beyond recognition.

THERE WAS A light on a chain in the powder room, and Reggie pulled the chain's fob as he leaned into the tarnished medicine cabinet mirror, opening his mouth wide and trying to examine his throat with the little flashlight, as he listened to make sure Florence wasn't still calling him to help set the table. He couldn't see anything inside the dark recess of his throat.

There was nothing in the powder room medicine cabinet except Band-Aids and Mercurochrome, a bottle of aspirin, and a box of hemorrhoid suppositories. On the back of the mirror, his mother had taped many years ago one of Dr. Henry's columns from the *Leader*. Reggie's mother had been dead for years, but neither he nor Florence had removed the clipping from the back of the mirror. The column was titled "The Seven Warning Signs of Cancer." People wrote letters to Dr. Henry and described their ailments and asked his professional opinion. "Dear Dr. Henry," every column began. "Dear Dr. Henry," this letter began, "please tell us the seven warning signs of cancer." The date was September 6, 1962. The newsprint was brown as a paper bag, and the Scotch tape at the top and bottom was brittle and yellow. After examining his throat, Reggie opened the cabinet and stared at the column:

The Seven Warning Signs of Cancer
1. appearance of a lump or growth on any part of the body
2. a sore that does not heal
3. sudden loss or gain in weight
4. change in the size, shape, or appearance of a mole
5. blood in the stool
6. difficulty swallowing or breathing
7. nagging cough or hoarseness

What Reggie feared was cancer of the larynx, the disease that had killed his father. Reggie's father had a laryngectomy in 1962 to remove his voice box. The operation included a tracheotomy, which left an opening in his throat that filled with mucus and had to be cleaned out often with a small suction machine like a dentist's.

From then on, Reggie's father — a man with a big baritone voice, a man who had loved joking and talking and singing — wore a strip of flannel around his neck and never spoke again. He kept in his shirt pocket a tiny notepad and a mechanical pencil and would "converse" in a kind of pictograph shorthand by writing quickly in his pad, tearing off the piece of paper, and handing it to whomever he was "speaking." Albert and Faye were little at the time and loved to participate in this communication. They would sit on the braided rug at the feet of the adults and courier their grandfather's notes, which, when directed to them, were more often than not tic-tac-toe.

After having lived in one side of the duplex for over twenty years, Reggie and Florence moved into Reggie's parents' side after his father died and his mother began to grow senile. For

Reggie it was a strange move, like going back in time, because he was moving back into the side of the duplex he had grown up in with his parents, his brother, Dorsey, his big sister, Bernadette, and his little sister, LaRue. Back then Uncle Stanley and Aunt Bertie lived in the other half of the duplex, which Reggie and Florence bought in the fifties after Aunt Bertie died.

Little by little after Reggie's father died, Reggie's mother worsened. At first she began to misplace things — her purse, her keys, her earrings — and to call Florence and Reggie by names they'd never heard before or names they recognized as those of distant or deceased relatives. One time Florence and Reggie went next door to help Reggie's mother find her purse — a large red bag with a shiny gold clasp like a scallop shell — and after an hour of searching, Reggie found the purse stuffed inside one of the refrigerator's crisper drawers.

Soon after that Reggie's mother baked a pie with nothing in it, and the crust caught on fire in the oven. Smoke filled the house and seeped next door, and Florence called the fire station while Reggie jumped across the common porch railing and saved his mother from smoke inhalation. Fire trucks came racing up the street, blowing their sirens and ringing their bells, the neighbors poured out of their houses like ants, and amidst all the hullabaloo, Reggie's mother kept accusing Florence of sneaking into her kitchen, scooping out the pie filling, and turning the oven temperature up to five hundred.

"She did it!" Reggie's mother hollered, pointing at Florence. "She's been stealing things from me and playing tricks on me for years. It's about time somebody did something about it."

It was then and there that Florence and Reggie began making plans to rent out their side of the duplex and move in with Reggie's mother, but just before they made the move, Reggie's mother disappeared. One April morning just before Easter, Reggie's mother arose before dawn, packed her small traincase, dressed in her best black dress, her Sunday shoes, Sunday coat, and Sunday hat, and walked downtown to the bus station where she bought a one-way ticket to Pittsburgh with the intent of visiting, they later learned, her youngest sister, Harriet. Harriet, however, had died from spinal meningitis in 1937. Reggie's mother was picked up two days after she disappeared. Someone in Pittsburgh had reported to the police that an old woman in a black coat and a peculiar black hat, an old woman with a black valise, had been sitting on a park bench like a statue for nearly twelve hours.

About a year after Florence and Reggie moved next door, Florence was in the kitchen dicing an onion for chili con carne when Reggie's mother came out of the powder room carrying a wad of soiled toilet paper. "Mummy," she said, tugging on Florence's apron, "what should I do with this?" Florence turned, her eyes full of onion tears, and Reggie's mother held the toilet paper in front of Florence's face. Seeing Florence's tear-stained face, Reggie's mother dropped the tissue and threw her arms around her.

"Oh don't cry, Mummy, don't cry," Reggie's mother said, as she began to sob uncontrollably herself.

Soon afterward, Reggie had his mother put in a nursing home, where she lived another three years, growing smaller and smaller, it seemed, every time they saw her. Her body seemed to flatten first, then disappear, making her head and hands appear large and dark against the white sheets, like Angry Jack's, and in her blue cotton nightgown she seemed to Reggie like a pitiful, discarded marionette from one of the puppet shows popular at carnivals when he was a boy.

When they moved in with Reggie's mother, Reggie and Florence left behind some old hand-me-down furniture — a blond veneer bedroom set, an old dining room table with five chairs and a wobbly buffet, a mohair couch and a matching overstuffed

chair, all of which had been Reggie's parents' — and rented the
house furnished. Tenants came and went, but for some time, an
Indian couple with a small boy named Bashir and a girl named
Saadia rented the duplex. The boy and girl were very close in
age, like Albert and Faye. Mr. Saeed was working on a Ph.D.
at the university, in chemical engineering, and Mrs. Saeed, who
always covered her hair with a scarf, worked in the university
library.

Reggie closed the medicine cabinet door quickly and
washed his hands. He held the pink bar of soap up to his nose
and closed his eyes. It was the brand of soap his mother had always kept in the powder room — Cashmere Bouquet — a cloying, flowery-smelling soap that filled the entire room, infusing
with its pink aroma the blue embroidered hand towel, the wallpaper with its Seven Wonders, the blue nubby fabric that covered the toilet seat, and the pages of the *Reader's Digest*s stacked
on the back of the tank. Although it was cold outside, Reggie
pushed the frosted window open the whole way — the custom-
ary gesture for airing out the powder room after a serious visit
— and unlocked the door.

As Reggie entered the kitchen, the doorbell rang. Albert,
Leslie, and their daughter, Victoria, all bearing packages, had
arrived for Christmas dinner. Florence was already hugging
Victoria while Leslie was unzipping the child's boots. Reggie
stooped to kiss the little girl and began to take everyone's coats
and hang them in the closet. He was always startled by how
much Victoria resembled Faye, and as he busied himself with
the coats, he blinked back tears. Victoria was five and flushed
with excitement. In one hand she held a round cardboard case
like an old-fashioned hatbox, painted metallic silver and with
the word *Cinderella* written in cursive pink glitter. Over a long-
sleeved Winnie-the-Pooh T-shirt, Victoria wore a blue satin

gown with white feathery fur around the collar and a matching short cape. Removing her pink Polarfleece hat, Victoria quickly opened her Cinderella box, added a tiara to her ensemble, and traded her snow boots for "glass" slippers.

Reggie and Florence had always hoped that Albert and Leslie would move next door — into the other half of the duplex, where Albert and Faye had been raised and where the Saeeds now lived. Lord knows they could have lived there for free; Reggie and Florence would have deeded it to them, and they could have remodeled it any way they saw fit. There was a nice front yard with an iron fence and gate and a side yard, too, a blue hydrangea and a pussy willow bush, a big silver maple. The old iron swing set was still there, and the clothesline, too, big enough for double sheets. There was even room to build on an extra bathroom, say, like a powder room under the stairs. There wasn't a garage, but there was always parking on the street or in the alley. And when children came along, why Florence and Reggie would be there to help out. Florence and Reggie had discussed the possibility excitedly when Albert announced his engagement to Leslie nearly ten years earlier.

"Imagine them, then," Florence said proudly, "starting out without a mortgage!" and Florence and Reggie decided then and there that they should invite Albert and Leslie to dinner so they could meet Leslie, who worked in the financial department of the same firm Albert worked for. They would have them to dinner, Florence and Reggie would, and make them their generous offer.

Albert and Leslie's courtship had been short, and Reggie and Florence had never met Leslie before Albert announced his engagement, although they had seen a picture of her once in an envelope of Kodak prints from Albert's company's picnic — a striking, athletic-looking brunette with a Dorothy Hamill haircut, holding a volleyball and standing in the center of a row of women in shorts and T-shirts bearing the company logo. Florence recognized her immediately when Albert escorted her through the door.

For dinner that first time Albert brought Leslie to meet his parents, Florence roasted a pork loin with apples and carrots, Vidalia onions, and new potatoes, and baked Boston brown bread to be served with Philadelphia cream cheese. Expensive canned asparagus. Celery hearts, miniature sweet gherkins, stuffed green olives, and jumbo pitted ripe ones served on Florence's mother's cut-glass relish tray. Leslie, however, did not eat meat or anything cooked in its juices. She was allergic to dairy products and had to avoid the olives, the pickles, and the asparagus because she was monitoring her sodium intake. She had a tendency, she explained, to retain water, and she was training for some kind of marathon. As Leslie nibbled on the celery, Albert ate heartily in the British style, never putting down his fork but holding it in his left hand with his index finger pressed firmly on the back of the tines, and eating from it like so. As he ate, he spelled out for Reggie and Florence his and Leslie's well-laid plans. Year one: a riverfront condo and scuba diving in Belize, money markets, stocks, and securities. Year two: a second car — a Volvo. Two children, one during year three, the other, year nine. Year six: a vacation home in the Poconos . . . Year twenty-two: early retirement. In between were Suzuki violin lessons for the children, Montessori and private schools, a small dog — possibly — for the children (a miniature dachshund, perhaps), skiing, and a trip abroad every third year. On and on Albert talked, and Leslie smiled and took tiny bites of celery, all the while adding details to Albert's monologue, saying, Albert, don't forget this, and Albert, don't forget that.

Every now and then, Florence nodded her agreement, smiled, and exclaimed, *How nice!* or *Oh my!* After a while, Reggie scratched behind his ear and turned off his hearing aid. The voices at the table became a low-pitched murmur, and the familiar high-decibel ring in Reggie's ears made its swift, familiar crescendo. Against the soothing, nearly inaudible symphony, hands and mouths moved as in a silent film, and in the dull thrum of gravity's pull, Reggie found himself thinking of Faye: Faye as a toddler in blue Dr. Denton pajamas; diapered Faye in the home movies, falling down on her behind with a silent plop; Faye, small and fiery Faye, out to save the world.

Behind Florence, on the dining room wall opposite from where Reggie sat, hung an old reverse painting on glass, which his mother had bought at the 1939 New York World's Fair. The painting was in a dark oval frame with curved glass and depicted the Statue of Liberty in New York Harbor, an American flag unfurling its forty-eight stars and thirteen stripes in the sky behind it. The folds of the statue's robe, the tips of her crown, portions of the torch, and some of the flag's stars were accented with paper-thin slivers of mother-of-pearl. The painting had always seemed to Reggie to be dark and flat and lacking color, but as the sun began to set and Albert talked on and on outside the range of Reggie's hearing, the statue came alive. Against the dark waters and foreboding Kerry-blue sky, the mother-of-pearl shimmered in the luminous folds of Liberty's gown and crown. The stars and torch twinkled pink and silver and pale blue.

There was pineapple upside-down cake for dessert, made the proper way — in an iron skillet — but Albert and Leslie had had to rush off, so there was no time at all to eat it, and the adjoining house was never mentioned.

TODAY, TAKING COATS and hats, Reggie noticed Albert's thinning hair. A few strands of dark hair were combed from one ear across the entire top of his head, plastered there securely somehow, and Reggie imagined them combed the other way, jutting stiffly out above his ear like a damaged, misplaced wing. A homely, impaired Mercury. Albert wore a prominent roll of fat around his middle, Reggie noticed, and when he turned around, his behind looked as wide and flat as a snow shovel. Leslie remained slim and trim, though, and Reggie knew Florence would secretly be scanning her body for signs of pregnancy. It had been Easter since they'd visited.

Reggie cleared his throat and made his greetings, marveling at how Victoria had grown, how well Albert and Leslie looked, how handsome their new Volvo. Every time Reggie spoke, a strange pressure seized his Adam's apple, making him feel as if he were choking. This unpleasant sensation had begun yesterday morning. Reggie was eating toast with orange marmalade, and suddenly he couldn't swallow. He spit out the toast, and all day he'd had trouble swallowing. He skipped lunch and dinner, telling Florence he just wasn't hungry. He said he'd had a big snack before lunch and another one right before dinner. All night he'd lain awake propped up on three pillows, because when he lay flat he was overcome with a panicky feeling that he couldn't swallow. Today he felt hoarser, and his voice was weak and shaky.

They sat in the sitting room — Reggie and Florence, Albert and Leslie, Victoria on the braided rug between them, examining and shaking the presents under the tree. When Florence announced that dinner would be ready in fifteen minutes, Reggie rose and said he had to go next door and check on the Saeeds' side, water their plants before he forgot again.

Every year, the Saeeds returned to Bombay over Christmas break, when the university was closed for a month. This year the Christmas holiday coincided with Ramadan. During Ramadan, Mr. Saeed explained to Florence and Reggie, you must fast all day until you cannot distinguish a white thread from a black thread by daylight. Then you may eat and drink small amounts at any time during the night, but when you can plainly distinguish a white thread from a black thread by daylight then the fast begins anew. After the last day of fasting — which lasts an entire month — gifts are exchanged and friends and family gather to pray and celebrate and eat big meals. The Saeeds would arrive in Bombay in time for Eid al-Fitr, the great Muslim feast marking the end of Ramadan, which took place this year on December 27.

"Can I go with you, Grandpa?" Victoria pleaded. What Reggie wanted was to be alone, maybe examine his throat again in the Saeeds' fluorescent bathroom light, but he could not say no to Victoria. Although he had seen very little of her, there was a peculiar bond between them, and everyone agreed that with her fair curly hair and narrow face, Victoria favored Reggie and Faye. Faye's and Victoria's baby pictures were almost indistinguishable.

Victoria bent her legs underneath her and curled her toes to keep a purchase on the glass slippers as Reggie lifted her over the common porch railing, as he had lifted his own children a thousand times in both directions, and as he had been lifted himself by his own father, going back and forth from Uncle Stanley and Aunt Bertie's. Reggie opened the aluminum storm door and unlocked the Saeeds' front door. They were greeted by the old two-ton, out-of-tune upright piano with its yellowed, broken keys; the nineteen-twenties mohair couch and overstuffed matching chair, pitifully sagging, which had belonged to Reggie's parents. No rugs, no lamps, just the dim overhead light. A lame card table by the couch where Reggie had stacked the Saeeds' mail. A Dr. Seuss book and a few plastic toys on the floor.

Victoria ran to the piano, losing en route a glass slipper, and with one finger began to pick out "Twinkle, Twinkle, Little Star." Reggie sat on the couch, sinking in deeply, and cleared his throat. He closed his eyes, and with his elbows on his knees, cradled his head in his hands. On the card table, the front page of yesterday's paper boasted "Lunar Eclipse on the Evening of December 25th; see story on page B-3."

It had been so long since Reggie had sat on the old mohair

couch, and as he sank in he remembered for a moment the couch being on the other side of the duplex when he was a boy, his parents sitting on it side by side, his mother always straightening the antimacassars, and other times — when his parents weren't home — jumping on the couch with his brother and sisters. One time they had jumped and jumped, and somehow from out of the couch's recesses surfaced a picture, a tiny framed photograph of a man they'd never seen. It was a black-and-white photo, a professional portrait, and the man in the picture was old and well-groomed, with slicked-back hair, bushy dark eyebrows, a crooked smile, a suit with wide lapels, and a funny kind of necktie. Reggie could see him even now. Who was he?

They never did identify him, but they named him "Couch Man," and whoever had the longest arm had stuffed him back into the couch's hinterlands. He remained with them, though, and for years they pretended that Couch Man was the boogieman who lived in the couch and ventured about at night when all the lights were out.

Couch Man! Dorsey would shout, jumping out from behind a door, or waiting in the dark among the Seven Wonders of the World, waiting for nature to call Reggie or Bernadette or little LaRue, then Dorsey leaping out of the powder room, scaring the living daylights out of one of them. As Reggie thought of his brother and sisters now, he reached his hand down the curved back and behind the cushions of the couch, down into the straw and the burlap webbing, and to his great surprise his fingertips came upon something cardboard, something velvety, something metal, something glass. As he drew out the photo, he noted, to his alarm, that Couch Man wasn't old at all. He was a young man. Much younger than Albert even. Younger, probably, than Faye was when she died. The photo was maybe taken for a high school yearbook, the young subject looking stiffer, older, and more stern than his years warranted, all in the typical portrait style of that era.

Reggie stared at the photo. After all these years, he thought, and still not a clue about who Couch Man might be. Just a man, an ordinary man, no doubt dead now, and here in his hand Reggie held a snapshot of him in his prime — a silver amalgam of all the dreams, all the hopes and secrets, all the possibilities of a life, captured in this tiny photograph. Just chemicals on paper, an image not faded in the least, buried all these years in darkness, in the stuffing of a couch. Whereas once he'd squealed and shivered at the name Couch Man, now Reggie felt ashamed. How strange and sad it seemed to hold in his palm this little face, the face of a dead man.

The lump in Reggie's throat seemed to thicken, heavy and burning like molten lead. Sadness burned in his chest and radiated down into his hands and up into his ears. His eyes burned, too, with the salty prelude to tears. Reggie closed his hands around the photograph and bowed his head. The sun was setting, and across the room at the piano, Victoria stood, her blue Cinderella gown shimmering like light on water. Outside the living room windows, the hillside began to glow pink in the twilight, and the windows of the houses across the river looked like minute chips of iridescent mica bursting into flames.

After a few rounds of "Twinkle, Twinkle" and a few unsuccessful bars of "We Three Kings," Victoria came and stood beside the couch. "Grandpa," Victoria said out of the blue, knocking playfully on the top of Reggie's lowered head with her small fist. "Grandpa, why doesn't Santa bring lots of toys to poor children?"

It was the big question, really, wasn't it? Reggie thought. It was the same thing Faye had wondered, too, when she was a little girl, a question she had asked many years before in this same room. Reggie's heart contracted. He looked up. He'd had no answer then, and he hadn't one now.

Through the common wall that joined the two houses, the voices of Florence and Albert and Leslie could be heard, and faintly the aroma of roasted turkey seeped into the Saeeds' side of the duplex. Far in the east, somewhere beneath the horizon, a black thread would soon be easily distinguishable from a white one, and the Saeeds would renew their fast. In the western hemisphere, the moon was rising, and the black shadow of the earth began to close over its white impassive face.

"I don't know, sweetheart," Reggie answered, and cleared his throat. "I don't know." He coughed and drew her to him. "But don't you ever forget that question," he added hoarsely. "Don't you ever forget it," he whispered, patting the child's small back.

The Pink Motel

LATELY, I HAVE BEEN thinking about becoming a Roman Catholic. The idea came to me last May while I was in Florence, guiding one of the Tuscany art tours for the agency, and while the others participated in the six-day death march/art fix — eight hours a day of walking, gaping, standing in museum lines, cramming all the glory of the Renaissance into forty-eight hours — I kept leaving the group, turning everything over to my assistant, and circling back to the Uffizi Gallery where we'd first begun. I was drawn there to room 15, the Leonardo da Vinci room, as if by some lodestone, and there I'd be, standing or sitting before the *Annunciation* as the tour went on without me. Slowly, there at the Uffizi, I began to think that religion — Catholicism — was what I needed. Faith. Mystery. Icons and saints. Rosaries, Hail Marys, Our Fathers. Forgiveness. Divine inspiration, and who knows? Maybe salvation, too, buried in the package like a Cracker Jack charm.

A Catholic! Yes, a Roman Catholic! With a catechism and an ecclesiastical calendar to guide me. A hierarchy of sins, holy days and saint's days, fasts and feasts. And a father, too. In absentia, true, but omnipresent nonetheless, hovering above me day and night like an invisible Goodyear blimp. Me, here on Earth, safe and sound in his umbra.

There in the Uffizi, before the *Annunciation,* as slowly the idea of conversion blossomed in me, I began to wonder if the impulse had not been in me all along and was only then making itself known in the voluminous folds of the Virgin's indigo gown, in the dimples of the beautiful angel curtsying before her. Such a beautiful, graceful messenger, bearing a time bomb, yes, but even so, curtsying and making the peace sign just the same — or was it the Brownie hello? — two fingers held up with his right hand. Such a lovely, curly-haired Gabriel who resembled, I imagined, a boy named Vincent whose ID bracelet I'd worn long ago.

MY FAMILY WAS not really religious. Oh, we said grace at Sunday dinner, and we observed in a secular way the Christian holidays — blue lights for advent, baked ham on Christmas, new hats for Easter. And there was a family Bible, too — from my mother's family, the Witherspoons — but we never read from it. I remember it mostly as a big black book with a peeling spine, a book whose pictures I enjoyed looking at with the same horror and thrill that I studied the illustrations in the Brothers Grimm. Daniel in the lion's den. Shadrach, Meshach, and Abednego huddled together in the fiery furnace. Lot's wife transformed into a pillar of salt. And poor Jonah, hunkered down and dismal in the belly of a whale. There was an illuminated fold-out family tree in the Bible, too, in which someone had written very carefully with a blue fountain pen the names of all the Witherspoons and their stitches of time, beginning at the trunk with someone named Hiram, and Fanny, his wife, and way up in the high boughs my cousins and me. The only other remarkable thing about the family Bible to me was Jesus's words in the New Testament: red as strawberry Twizzlers.

When I was around the age of three, my mother taught me to kneel by my bed and say my prayers while she sat on the bed's edge, knitting: *Now I lay me down to sleep* . . . I'd sing-say to the metronome of her needles, followed by the whole kit and caboodle of God bless so-and-sos, down to Pomp and Circumstance, the Woolworth's turtles my mother had named, which lived on my dresser in a shallow plastic bowl with a palm tree. I could not say "circumstance," so I called them Pomp and Underpants.

After these syncopated prayers, my mother would tuck me in and read to me about Brer Rabbit, Little Black Sambo, or Peter Pan, and then she'd kiss me on my forehead and turn out the light. Sometimes in the darkness, alone in my room, I'd hear a tiny bell ring and see a small light flicker about the ceiling and know it was Tinkerbell . . . until some time later, that is, when I came upon the penlight and cat bell in the pocket of my mother's dressing gown.

We were Protestants, but we paid allegiance to no particular denomination. Our commitments lay with the choir — the best choir — and we changed churches often, flitting from Presbyterian to Episcopalian to Lutheran to Methodist like bees among the thistles, searching always for a better choir, a better choir director, a better organist, a better libretto of anthems, a need for a contralto soloist, and most importantly, a choir and congregation that were truly appreciative of my mother's trained voice.

We avoided the Baptists on the grounds, I believe, that they sang what my mother considered a bastardized version of "Onward Christian Soldiers," the hymn she used as a litmus test of a church's musical acumen. The original — the Welsh version — was up-tempo, cut time, and victorious, rather jolly even, with a refrain where a tenor could clear his pipes, so to speak, but the Baptists sang a slower version in common time and repeated one note like a dirge, a rendition my mother found plodding and glum.

When we finally chose a church, the choir director — male or female — was swiftly seduced by my mother's voice, and she was doted on as an angel sent to grace the loft. As she performed her repertoire of solos Sunday after Sunday: "I Wonder as I Wander," "I Know That My Redeemer Liveth," "I Heard a Forest Praying" . . . I proudly beamed from my pew and sang along, while the other female choir members looked down with chagrin. My favorite solo of my mother's was "There Is a Balm in Gilead," which I imagined as the score to a Bugs Bunny cartoon, the homonymous "bomb" being a black cannonball with a sizzling fuse, Gilead a rabbited Dogpatch. After a few months, we would move on to another church, another denomination, another choir with its sourpuss altos and sopranos.

My mother, I learned from Aunt Dizzy when she came to stay, had yearned to be a professional singer when she was young. She dreamed of starring in operettas and Broadway musicals and gay cabarets, but war was imminent, and her father frowned upon her aspirations as frivolous, and so she became something sensible — a nurse — and served in the Red Cross in New Zealand where Aunt Dizzy introduced her to my father, an American serving with the Navy. My father, Aunt Dizzy said, had wanted to join a traveling circus in his youth, but the outbreak of World War II, and *his* father, she said, had sobered him up relentlessly, too.

AFTER THE WAR, my father became a drummer — a traveling salesman for the Fuller Brush Company. Personable and charismatic, Walter Jones worked as a front man, covering a territory for a year, then, when the customer base was established, moving on to develop another base in the next Fuller Brush region, hiring local men called trainees to expand the business he had begun, serving the customers he had won over to the wonderful world of Fuller brushes. And so our little family swept across the United States like one of Alfred C. Fuller's guaranteed brooms.

I was born in St. Louis during one of my father's eastward sweeps, and by the time I was six — when my father disappeared — we were living in Zanesville, Ohio. The last time my father was seen alive was at a Catholic school in Indian Creek, Pennsylvania, where he demonstrated to several nuns and a deaf-mute custodian the wonders and versatility of his wares. These wares included brushes of all sorts and sizes, brooms and mops and dust cloths, commercial detergents and disinfectants, spot removers, polishes, and waxes, all tucked away in his demonstration case like clowns in a Mini Cooper. My father's Fuller Brush case was large and black, full of compartments, drawers, and leather straps. It opened up into a kind of stage with tiers and graduated wings, like a cross between a steamer trunk, a puppet theater, and a humongous jewelry box.

The case is in my attic, and though nearly fifty years have passed since he used it, it remains virtually untouched since the day he disappeared — a young man, I know now, although at the time of his disappearance, forty seemed to me very old. I don't remember much about my father, only that he was a big man (as all adults must have seemed to me then) with a shock of red, curly hair like Danny Kaye, which I held on to for dear life when he carried me on his shoulders. There were photographs, too, from which I could construct certain scenes until they became part of my memory: standing with my father in front of a war memorial with a biplane, and on the steps of a narrow brick house with my mother there, too, in a hat like a dinner plate and a dark flared coat with a big corsage — a peony or aster perhaps — pinned to it, and me on my father's shoulders. Just those few snapshots and little things he said and did. For instance, he could juggle: oranges and crookneck squashes, eggplants and zucchini. And if you sneezed, he would say with a funny accent, *'it 'im agin, 'e's an Irishman!* And if you said, *Ya know what?* my father would snap back, *Why, he invented the steam engine, did he not?* It was an old joke that made a wordplay on the surname of James Watt, who was often credited with having invented the high-pressure steam engine in 1769.

I remember that when my father came home, sometimes after an entire week on the road, he always rang the doorbell, and when my mother answered, he'd say in his very proper Fuller Brush man's voice, *Is the lady of the house at home?* and my mother would say very sternly in an affected cockney sort of accent, *We don't want any,* and slam the door, and we'd stand there giggling behind it — my mother and I — our hands over our mouths, until the bell rang again, and then there would be a great deal of hugging and kissing and laughing, and my father would chase me through the house, lumbering after me like a clumsy giant and calling out in a booming voice, *When I catch that little Fanny, I'll gobble her up!* or *Come here, you little scalawag!* I'd squeal and dart around the furniture, and when my father caught me he'd swing me up so high I could touch the ceiling, and when he put me down, I'd rummage through his coat pockets, which always held a box of Cracker Jacks or Chiclets and sometimes something else, too: a plastic whistle shaped like a bird or a tin pocket cricket.

Some of my fondest memories of my mother date back to these days before I was old enough to go to school, to the time before my father disappeared and we went to live with Aunt Dizzy. Before that time, I had my mother all to myself, and we spent the days alone while my father was on the road peddling his Fuller Brush wares. But in spite of these good times with my mother, there were other times that were upsetting. On two occasions after awakening from a nap, I couldn't find my mother. I tiptoed through the house from room to room, quietly calling her name. One time I found her sitting at the kitchen table, crying. Her head was on her arms, which were folded atop an open photo album. The other time she was lying on my parents' bed in her slip, the blinds drawn tight, sobbing into a pillow. In the darkened room, the afternoon light peeped through the edge of the blinds and made a row of dots like a string of pearls across her shoulders. Although my mother quickly recovered when she saw me standing in the doorway and made me a treat — tapioca pudding with canned mandarin oranges, which I loved so much — these scenes have haunted me since, though I never mentioned them to her as long as she lived.

To MY FATHER's Fuller Brush display case in my attic, I have made only one alteration: the addition of a prayer card of Saint Anthony the Abbot, which I got from Ruby Reese in the sixth grade, trading away a pair of hand-knitted blue angora mittens, which, with a guilty conscience, I told my mother I had lost. The prayer card, brown around the edges now like a piece of toast, shows Saint Anthony looking very much like an anorexic Santa Claus, holding a staff with a cross on top and a tiny bell, and surrounded by pigs. I wanted the card because it was holy — although I wasn't entirely certain what "holy" meant, but I knew it was special — and because it bore a connection to my father who was last seen at St. Anthony the Abbot Catholic School for Boys and Girls. The more I looked at the card, the more I began to imagine that the man in the pastel drawing was not really a saint named Anthony at all, but my father, Walter Meriwether Jones.

From the back of the card, I learned that at the age of twenty, Saint Anthony the Abbot gave away everything he owned and moved alone to the eastern Sahara Desert, where he lived out the remaining eighty-three years of his life in an abandoned Roman fort. Although he tried to be a hermit, pilgrims from all over sought him out, and he ministered to them and healed them miraculously, without even trying. So many disciples arrived and settled where Anthony had holed up that eventually a monastery was founded there on the banks of the Nile. Many of Saint Anthony's followers supported themselves by making baskets and brushes, and from that he came to be known as the patron saint of basketweavers and brushmakers. His relationship to swine is less obvious, but possibly because brushes are made from boar bristles, swine herders also took him as their patron saint — thus the pigs surrounding him on the prayer card. For reasons even less obvious, he is also the patron saint of gravediggers, epileptics, and those afflicted with skin diseases, especially one extremely itchy and inflammatory disorder called erysipelas, similar to shingles and commonly known as Saint Anthony's fire.

From the *Encyclopedia Britannica* in our public library, I learned that Saint Anthony lived to be one hundred three and that every single day of his long life was a never-ending struggle against the devil. Satan's assault on Anthony took the form of seductive and horrible visions. Sometimes when Anthony was fasting, a monk would appear offering bread, and when Anthony politely refused, the monk took great offense and beat him to a pulp. At other times the devil appeared in the form of wild beasts, brutal soldiers, or bare naked women who taunted him and whipped him and ripped his flesh, sometimes leaving him near death. Those who witnessed these attacks were convinced they were real, although they themselves never saw the perpetrators, only Saint Anthony tussling alone like a shadow boxer in a carnival sideshow.

Sometimes I would take the prayer card from its secret hiding place under the red velvet lining of my jewelry box and stare at it, trying to imagine my father as Saint Anthony, fighting off wild animals and demons like Prince Valiant or Captain Marvel.

THE DAY MY father disappeared was Tuesday, February 21, 1956, the day before George Washington's birthday. Just before lunch, the sky darkened so that it seemed almost nightfall as a storm blew in off the Great Lakes and swept down through the flat Ohio plains. Sleet slapped so hard against our classroom windows that we could hardly hear our first-grade teacher, Mrs. Truman, speak. We were frightened, and Mrs. Truman, who always wore brown and was shaped like a hen — with a big front and even bigger bottom and a sway to her back that made her seem to always be leaning forward, about to peck at something — gathered us around her in our little reading circle at the front of the room, where we sat in our baby-bear chairs, holding our readers in our laps. The fluorescent lights flickered as we read aloud about young George Washington with his tricorn hat and his ax, and while we read, the sleet turned to snow, and in no time everything was encrusted in a stiff white meringue, and objects in the playground gradually began to appear as large pieces of a kind of white candy I was particularly fond of, a confection called divinity.

By late afternoon, the sun was shining, although the temperature remained below freezing, and everyone was happy again. Back in our regular rows, I forgot all about the black clouds and the ice storm, and I began to daydream about the cherry pie my mother would soon be baking to celebrate George Washington's birthday: canned, stoned cherries under a lattice crust and a scoop of Dolly Madison vanilla ice cream melting alongside each slice.

When school let out, there was my mother standing in the playground in her winter coat with the pile lining, a plaid wool scarf tied under her chin babushka style. We walked home, slipping and sliding all the way, and stopped at the A&P to buy the can of pie cherries and four pork chops, none of which she ever cooked. All evening we sat on the davenport, holding back the sheers and looking out the front window, but my father never came home.

I must have fallen asleep, and someone must have carried me upstairs, because I awoke the next morning in my own bed. From the landing, I heard unfamiliar voices, and when I peeped over the railing, I saw the hall light reflected in the shiny patent leather visor of a policeman's cap. Neighbors came and went, and my mother sat by the phone for days. My father was never found, nor his car, although a few days later, his Fuller Brush case turned up, unharmed in spite of the weather, just off the shoulder of a secondary road a few miles from Niagara Falls.

After my father disappeared, my mother grew sullen. She stopped knitting and singing in the church choir and reading to me at bedtime, and I, in turn, stopped saying my prayers. Tinkerbell no longer visited my room at night, and one day when I went to pick up Pomp, his shell came off in my hand. The bowl was dry, with just a sticky brown ring where the water had been, and Underpants, likewise, was dead.

My mother had taken to staying in bed most of the time, with the venetian blinds drawn, getting up only to use the bathroom or open a can of soup. She would wake me in the morning and tell me to get myself dressed, and then she'd go back to bed. I would make some toast and drink a big glass of chocolate milk and walk to school, and when I came home she would still be in bed in her blue bed jacket.

Then Aunt Dizzy came. Aunt Dizzy's real name was Dolores, but she never went by that. Everyone called her Dizzy. She had skin the color of buckwheat honey and curly hair like a poodle. She was tall and skinny and what I would describe today as wiry. She smoked Lucky Strikes and wore baggy trousers and shoes without socks or stockings in all weather, and men's cologne called Clubman Lilac Vegetal. It was when Aunt Dizzy stayed with us in Zanesville, Ohio, that I found the bell and penlight in the pocket of my mother's robe, although I did not immediately put two and two together.

AUNT DIZZY KNEW nothing about disciplining children. She was a very busy person, and for the most part ignored me, spending her time cleaning and washing, ironing and knitting, and taking things upstairs to my mother, like Salada tea with fortunes on the tag, oyster crackers, Jello, and chicken gumbo soup. Her response to any request I made was *Does your mother let you do that?* or *Does your mother let you have that?* and she accepted my answers unequivocally. Under Aunt Dizzy's supervision, I ate bowl after bowl of Neapolitan ice cream, serving myself as I pleased, and drinking Hershey's syrup out of the can with a straw. I did not wear underpants or shoes. I was allowed to crack half a dozen eggs on the sidewalk in front of our house and swish them around with a spatula after overhearing a neighbor say that it was hot enough to fry an egg on the pavement. Flies and ants converged on the mess, which a neighborhood dog — a little pug named Churchill — came along and made short work of.

Under Aunt Dizzy's supervision, I could stay up as late as I wanted and watch Jack Benny and Groucho Marx on television, and even later, blurry eyed, until the national anthem, station identification, and the bull's-eye came on. During the day, I roamed the neighborhood far and wide, opening gates and traipsing through strangers' yards, picking their peonies and irises, and twisting off low branches of flowering shrubs, all of which I proudly carried home to my mother without any inquiries from Aunt Dizzy as to where or how I acquired such ragged bouquets. On the contrary, Aunt Dizzy praised me for my thoughtfulness.

During Aunt Dizzy's stay in Zanesville, I discovered that I could walk the few blocks to Bobette's Confectionery and just stand beside the ice cream cooler looking forlorn, and in no time at all someone would buy me a Dixie cup or a Dreamsicle, or Bobette herself would just give me one. The end to my wanderings and adventures came about when I was escorted home in a police cruiser after riding my bicycle — with its training wheels — down the shoulder of Highway 62, wearing only my pajamas, heading for nowhere in particular.

When I reflect on this behavior, it is hard for me to imagine that I, an inherently shy, even demure child, acted out so during this time. Perhaps because intellectually I could not process the concept of loss, it made itself known to me at a baser — a molecular — level and traveled through my cells, working itself slowly through my entire body like the needle in the story Aunt Dizzy used to tell about the sixteen-year-old bride who stepped on a fine needle while sewing her trousseau, and the needle emerged from a tear duct in the corner of her eye as she lay dying at age ninety-three. For some time after my father's disappearance, I was naughty and angry and did horrible things, although I managed to maintain an angelic façade in front of my mother and Aunt Dizzy. Eventually I found other, more acceptable outlets for my grief.

ONE VERY HOT night during this time when Aunt Dizzy lived with my mother and me in Zanesville, I woke up and heard first just the cicadas singing. I opened my ears, and across the hallway I heard my mother crying, softly at first, and then more loudly until it became a wail. I lay in my own bed, crying too, wishing for my father to come home and ring the doorbell, for the times when I said my prayers and my mother sat on my bed and read to me, and for the nights when Tinkerbell flitted about my room. By this time I had figured out the Tinkerbell charade and kept the penlight and the bell under my own pillow in a little suede pouch that Aunt Dizzy had given me.

I lay there on my back crying, tears puddling in the shells of my ears, and when I rolled over and reached to turn my pillow over to its cool side, there were the Tinkerbell things — the bell and penlight — so I tiptoed out into the hall with them and to the doorway of my mother's room. On my parents' bed lay my mother and Aunt Dizzy, naked, holding each other. The covers were all tousled and my mother was still sobbing. Aunt Dizzy was stroking my mother's hair. I crouched in the doorway and jingled the little cat bell in my fist and blinked the penlight on and off up on the ceiling like my mother used to do.

Come here, you little scalawag, my mother said to me, pulling the covers up over herself and Aunt Dizzy, and I crawled in beside her and fell fast asleep.

Soon after that we dragged everything in the house in Zanesville out to the backyard and had a grand sale with lemonade and a cigar box full of quarters and dollar bills, and then we drove in Aunt Dizzy's DeSoto "back home."

Back home was a place called Ashport where Aunt Dizzy had grown up. In Ashport, Aunt Dizzy, my mother, and I lived comfortably in a narrow row house, and I recognized the stoop as the one in the photograph of my mother, my father, and me. The house was not brick at all but covered all over with a kind of roof shingle that looked from a distance like sooted brick but up close resembled sandpaper and sparkled in the sun. In Ashport we had a player piano, and my room had pink-and-white-striped wallpaper and a window that looked out on the alley, and a high-up shelf where I lined up all my dolls. Aunt Dizzy and my mother shared the front room, which was bigger and papered with yellow roses and shaded by one of many ginkgo trees that lined Diamond Avenue. In the summer, in the evenings, I played hide-and-seek in the cemetery across the

street, calling out *olly olly oxen free* or hiding behind angels, sep-
ulchers, and obelisks, while the mothers of the children I played
with walked along the paths in twos or threes, their arms linked
together, fireflies blinking in the grass and flickering amidst
the tombstones, and sometimes Aunt Dizzy and my mother
walked, too.

In Ashport, my mother seemed more like her old self. Doilies
began to appear here and there on the arms of chairs, and then
she started singing (although never again in a choir), and before
long, she began to put on a starched blue uniform in the morning and ride a streetcar into another part of town where Aunt
Dizzy had gotten her a job caring for a rich sick man in his
home, which was the kind of nursing Aunt Dizzy did, too.

As time passed, we spoke less and less of my father until
eventually his name was rarely mentioned. Only Aunt Dizzy
spoke of him, and only when she and I were alone, drying dishes
or folding clothes. Then she would tell me things about him.
Just little things he'd said and done. She never referred to him as
Walter but said, *Your father* . . . and she said this in such a hushed
way it was almost as if she were about to recite the Lord's Prayer
in the second person. Aunt Dizzy had grown up with my father,
and she told me how one summer he strung a cable between two
trees in his yard and day after day practiced tightrope walking,
using a heavy wooden curtain rod as a balance pole or holding
his father's black umbrella as he walked back and forth, wob-
bling, one bare foot placed carefully in front of the other.

Two framed photographs of my father sat on top of the
player piano, which occupied a wall of our dining room. One
was a large tinted photo of him in a white uniform and cap, his
lips and cheeks pink as bubble gum, his eyes a startling blue.
The other photo was the one of my father with me on his shoulders, my mother standing beside us, wearing the cabbage-size
corsage. When I was home alone, I would sometimes sit on the
piano bench and take one or the other of the photographs down

and stare at it with my eyes wide open until they began to smart, and once the tears began, I would clutch the photo to my chest like I had seen Judy Garland do in a movie, pressing a photo of Clark Gable to her bosom and singing "You Made Me Love You."

Daddy, Daddy, I'd sniffle. On the wall adjacent to the piano was the sideboard with its long, low mirror and plate rail, and if I turned my head slightly, I could see my grievous self reflected amid the Blue Willow cups and saucers.

THE SUMMER I was ten, I rode with my mother to Indian Creek, Pennsylvania — the last place my father was seen alive. It had been four years since my father had disappeared. In the summer, on my mother's day off from work, we often took Aunt Dizzy's car and drove to a small amusement park not far away, where my mother liked to sit in her sundress and read magazines by the pool while I splashed in the shallow end because I couldn't swim. When I tired of that, I rode the kiddie rides, which I was really too big for but preferred just the same: the gigantic cups and saucers that spun this way and that, and the little boats that made their way through a moat of ankle-deep water.

This day, though, my mother drove past the entrance to the park and kept going. She had packed Velveeta cheese sandwiches and a bag of Wise potato chips, and we had a thermos of Hawaiian Punch. I asked where we were going, but all she said was *You'll see.* We drove by the world's largest teacup, which wasn't so big after all, and down a white bumpy highway along a river until we came to an Indian burial mound and the town of Indian Creek. In a small, tree-lined parking lot next to St. Anthony the Abbot Church, we sat in Aunt Dizzy's car staring at the school across the street. The building was Gothic and imposing: dark cut stone like a fortress and with a slate roof and what seemed like hundreds of pigeons cooing and fluttering about.

Above the door's curved arch, in raised letters, I read, SAINT AN-THONY THE ABBOT CATHOLIC SCHOOL FOR BOYS AND GIRLS. No one was around. My mother got out and crossed the street and walked up the spooned-out steps and tried the door. She put her hands to the glass and peered in and then walked around to a side door, which also was locked.

For an hour or so, we slowly drove up and down the streets of Indian Creek. Down the main street we went and past the ra-dio station where the country music stars played and by a neigh-borhood playground and two small cemeteries and along the or-dinary streets and alleys. Often my mother bent low over the steering wheel so she could see out my window to the other side of the street, up a set of porch steps. I would have been bored were it not that there was something mysterious about the day, which I relished, and I enjoyed the change of scenery, the way the skyline fell away as we drove south along the white, rhyth-mic road, the lazy river winking beside us, its banks strewn with smokestacks and the low, garbled hulk of glass factories.

We stopped once at a park along the river and bought ice cream from a Good Humor man, and my mother talked with him a long time as I licked my cone and twirled on a nearby swing. A few miles outside town, near a place called Indian Lake, there was a carnival with a ferris wheel. It was still after-noon, and there would not be much activity until evening. I rode a pony around and around a circle while a boy not much older than I held the reins, and my mother talked at length to a slov-enly man in a Porky Pig hat. On the way back home, my mother made me promise not to tell Aunt Dizzy where we had been, and when Aunt Dizzy came home that evening, she never asked me what we did that day, so there was really nothing not to say.

IT WAS IN Ashport that I met my aunt Mary Alice and my only cousins, Eugene and Ralphie, whose names were inked in on the same limb as mine on the Witherspoon family tree. Eugene and Ralphie were identical twins four years older than me. Their father, my mother's older brother, Eugene, had been killed in Iwo Jima when Eugene and Ralphie were only babies. They lived in Cleveland, Ohio, but stopped once in Ashport to see us when they were on their way to an identical twins convention in Philadelphia.

Aunt Mary Alice's eyebrows were plucked and then drawn on with a very thin pink pencil. Her hennaed hair she wore in a good-sized lump that stuck out over her forehead like a liverwurst. She wore a black crêpe de Chine dress, shorter than the dresses my mother wore, with larger-than-life-size irises printed on it, and she had remarried — someone named Mr. Michael Georgianus, CPA, who had his name printed on a business card, which Aunt Mary Alice proudly presented to my mother. The twins were dressed alike in blue blazers with gold anchors on the buttons. Eugene and Ralphie were ugly and obnoxious — one of them would have been too many. They resembled Sluggo from *Nancy* in the funny papers, and they were impossible to tell apart. Even Aunt Mary Alice said so.

After Aunt Mary Alice introduced them, she said to my mother, "And this must be your little Fanny," which sent Eugene and Ralphie into a fit of laughing hysterics. They sat side by side on our wicker settee — Eugene and Ralphie — and one of them picked his nose almost incessantly. Every time they looked at me or someone said my name, Eugene and Ralphie started laughing, and Aunt Mary Alice boxed their ears. They were both poking at each other all the time and giggling. The nonpicker kept saying, "So, Fanny . . . ," and then they would both burst out laughing, leaning over and holding their bellies and then throwing themselves back and kicking out their feet, almost toppling over our little settee, while Aunt Mary Alice apologized, saying, "Don't pay them any mind, Fanny dear," which inspired even more of their hateful snickers.

I was used to this kind of mockery about my name, especially from boys, the whole lot of whom I found disgusting. After a short time, I asked my mother if I could be excused. As I skipped upstairs, I heard Aunt Mary Alice tell my mother how lucky she was to have a girl. In my mother and Aunt Dizzy's room, I removed the Witherspoon family Bible from their dresser and immediately tried to erase Eugene and Ralphie's names from the family tree. I did this by licking a stale pencil eraser — which I had seen my mother do to erase fountain-pen ink — and rubbing, but in my efforts, the names were removed not by an erasure exactly, but rather, a good-sized hole.

Soon after their visit, Aunt Mary Alice, Eugene, Ralphie, and Mr. Michael Georgianus, CPA, moved to North Carolina, and I never saw any of them again until many years later when Aunt Mary Alice showed up at my mother's funeral. By that time, she had grown to be a woman of truly ponderous proportions, leaning on a black cane, still with pink eyebrows and the most peculiar color hair, although her hair was short then and teased into a muffin shape. From the neck up, she reminded me of a kind of puffed-up sea urchin I had seen once in the Pittsburgh aquarium. It was Aunt Mary Alice who had called my mother about five years after her visit with Eugene and Ralphie to tell her that she had seen my father. Yes, she said, she was absolutely certain it was him or she wouldn't have called.

We were eating dinner when the phone rang. "Fanny," my mother said to me, standing in the doorway and holding the receiver against her chest, "go to your room."

I pushed my chair back from the table and stood up, but I lingered there and sat down again, listening, and my mother let me stay. I was, after all, nearly twelve. My mother motioned to Aunt Dizzy, who got up from the table and went over to the phone stand and listened with her head against my mother's, the receiver pressed between their ears like a black kitten.

A few days later, we packed a cooler with sandwiches and

Fig Newtons, filled the big thermos with iced tea, and headed south in Aunt Dizzy's DeSoto. Aunt Dizzy and my mother took turns driving and navigating, one of them always holding the road map on her lap and tracing our route with an eyebrow pencil. I lay stretched out on the backseat, sometimes with my feet out the window, watching the clouds and the telephone poles fly by. After nightfall, a mist rose up and filled the valleys and swirled around the mountains. We drove over Indian Gap Mountain and down into West Virginia, through the Monongahela National Forest and down the Blue Ridge Mountains, where we saw a mother bear and her cub standing nonchalantly by the roadside as if waiting for a bus.

I knew quite well where we were going and why, but Aunt Dizzy and my mother didn't talk about it. We pretended to be on a splendid vacation, singing along with Patsy Cline and the Everly Brothers on the radio and playing guessing games like Twenty Questions. It was the first time I had gone anywhere of any distance since we moved to Ashport, other than once to a funeral in Ohio and another time with the Brownies to see Niagara Falls. Night fell, and we kept driving. Somewhere we passed a motel with a neon sign displaying a fairy that looked like Tinkerbell, with blinking pink wings and a blinking magic wand. I had never stayed in a motel, and I begged my mother to stop at the Pink Motel, but she drove on by, saying it was nearly morning and it was too expensive and we were almost there.

"There" was a small town in North Carolina, where we had breakfast at a shiny diner and took turns in the tiny ladies' room, brushing our teeth and freshening up. We spent the better part of the day in a small park along a river, napping on knitted afghans under a sycamore tree and eating bloated hotdogs purchased from a street vendor. Across the river, a carnival was setting up, and when the colored lights came on in the early afternoon and the ferris wheel began to turn, we walked along the river and across a low concrete bridge and entered the fair through a garish, arched gateway.

My mother wore sunglasses and a scarf printed with portraits of the presidents tied about her hair and under her chin like Sophia Loren; Aunt Dizzy wore her Panama hat. We walked up and down the midway lined with food booths and tables with silver and turquoise jewelry, baseball cards, and pocketknives. There were ring toss games and pop bottles to be broken with a baseball; goldfish and stuffed animals and glass walking sticks to be won; portrait painters and a fortuneteller; a puppet show; and a freak show that boasted a lobster boy, a bearded lady, and a calf with two heads. I begged to have my fortune told, but my mother forbid it. Aunt Dizzy, though, entered a tent with a beaded curtain for a door and came out a few minutes later, shaking her head.

I SAW HIM first, I think, but maybe my mother had already spotted him through the crowd. He was dressed like a pirate with a blousy shirt and a red sash, a black bandanna wrapped tightly around his head. He had a waxed handlebar mustache and a patch over one eye. He was big and impressive and stood with his arms crossed, like Mr. Clean. There was a tall boy about my age, with broad shoulders and a downy mustache — a smaller version of the older man — who was dressed similarly with the exception of a Zorro hat instead of a bandanna, and between them they began juggling Indian clubs.

Inside the circle formed by the crowd stood a buxom woman dressed in a long, colorful, but dirty skirt, flounced and tiered like a gypsy's. She had a broad, pretty face, but one of her front teeth was missing. She wore a peasant blouse and gold hoop earrings, and her hair was pulled back in a straggly braid. Her eyes were as black as ripe olives. She tossed the clubs, more and more of them, into the air between them.

They juggled expertly, putting on a fancy act like on the *Ed Sullivan Show,* catching clubs behind their backs and under their legs and changing places, throwing the clubs higher and higher, the woman adding more until it seemed inevitable that one of them would miss and there would be a great tumbling collision of clubs in the air between them. But they never missed, and if he saw us in the crowd, he didn't show it. The audience applauded, the jugglers bowed, and then they juggled fiery batons, which the gypsy woman set aflame by dipping them into a bucket of something flammable and passing them, with a whoosh, through the flame of a standing torch.

A dark girl, perhaps age seven or eight, walked around the rim of the crowd, collecting coins in a galvanized bucket. After the juggling, the man who may have been my father leaned way back and swallowed swords and extinguished flaming pokers in his mouth. All the while the crowd winced and said, *Aaagh!* and turned away and quickly back again. Off to the side, a smaller girl of five or six stood in a loose, soiled dress, holding a jar of soapsuds and a wire wand, blowing bubbles. It was she who captured my attention. She looked right at me and our gazes locked for a moment before she turned her attention back to her jar. We had the same features, the same wide, thin-lipped mouth and deep-set, heavy-lidded eyes, the same curly hair, although she was small and dark-complected, and I was much taller and fair, a redhead, like my father.

The sword swallower looked nothing like the figure of Saint Anthony the Abbot on the prayer card, the emaciated figure who for years I had imagined as my father. Neither did he bear resemblance to the man in the photograph holding me on his shoulders, nor the cadet with cheeks and lips as pink as Pepto-Bismol, and although I had felt an excited apprehension, an unfamiliar nervousness like a jittery creature inside me throughout the entire trip from Ashport to North Carolina, I suddenly felt quite numb, as if I were not a part of any of it, just an observer, large and invisible — a tourist at the Pittsburgh aquarium staring from behind a glass wall at a school of exotic fish, or maybe one of the fishes, staring back at the people.

My mother stood beside me, transfixed. *Walter?* she whispered to no one in particular. She was trembling. We were some ways back in the crowd, and the low sun was blinding. When she said my father's name, though, which I had not heard her speak in many years, I was pulled into the here and now. I stared at the sword swallower. I observed his hands, his shoulders, his arms, his lips closing around the flames. I knew it was him, but my attention was drawn completely to the dark little girl with the bubbles, who looked like a wallet-size negative of me.

It was Aunt Dizzy who led my mother away, taking her by the arm and heading down the midway. My mother's straw purse hung limply from her hand, and she walked the listless, mechanical stride of a sleepwalker. I started after them, my heart pounding, but I stumbled in the dirt, and when I turned and looked back, I saw that the little girl with the bubbles had followed after me and now stood almost beside me.

"Ya know what?" she looked up and said to me, and I said, without even thinking, something I had not heard or said in many years: "Why, he invented the steam engine, did he not?"

The girl's eyes widened and her jaw dropped. Her hand flew up over her mouth. She dropped the glass jar of bubbles, turned, and ran back to the dirt circle where the juggling had resumed, and disappeared.

"It's not him, Sissy," Aunt Dizzy was saying to my mother when I caught up with them. She had her arm around my mother's waist and had taken her purse from her.

"Listen to me, Sissy, it's not him," Aunt Dizzy said again and again.

My mother looked pale beyond belief, and I can still see her face as it was then, her dark glasses removed and the pinkish faces of half a dozen dead presidents on her headscarf framing her own white face like lightbulbs around a starlet's dressing room mirror. Outside the fairgrounds, we sat for a long while on a bench along the river, none of us speaking, Aunt Dizzy in the middle with one arm around my mother, the other arm around me. The red sun was setting as we began driving north, Aunt Dizzy at the wheel, and before long, a heavy fog rose up and swallowed the black road wiggling through the Blue Ridge Mountains.

We slept that night in the Pink Motel, in a room with two double beds. There were pink chenille bedspreads on the beds and between them a nightstand with a pink princess phone, and in the bathroom miniature bars of pink Cashmere Bouquet soap no bigger than a business card, a glittery pink and gold plastic shower curtain, a pink commode, a pink bathtub, and a pink sink — all in various shades of pink and a rosy-beige color popular back then, which was called desert sand. My mother lay down on top of one of the beds and fell asleep almost immediately, and I took a shower just for the novelty of it because we didn't have a shower at home, and then I stared at myself for a long time in the streaky medicine cabinet mirror. When I came out of the bathroom, my mother was under the covers.

Aunt Dizzy and I played Crazy Eights at a wobbly table by the window and drank Coca-Colas out of glasses filled with ice from a sparkly pink ice bucket, another object I'd never seen before. The curtains were drawn and through the thin, nubby fabric and the heavy fog, the neon outline of the fairy on the motel sign was just visible, blinking on and off.

Sitting there that night in the Pink Motel, with my mother sound asleep and Aunt Dizzy and I laying down our cards, Aunt Dizzy smoking her Lucky Strikes, I knew I didn't want that big fire-eating, sword-swallowing man to come join us in Ashport. I didn't want him sitting at our dining room table and sleeping with my mother in the room with yellow roses. I didn't want him to be my father. And those other people — the big boy, the gypsy woman with the missing tooth, the dirty girl collecting coins, the little girl in the shabby dress who looked so much like me — I didn't want them looking in our windows, knocking on our door. That night in the Pink Motel, I was happy. The crude jokes that boys like Eugene and Ralphie always made about my name and the things I knew kids in school whispered behind my back about my mother and Aunt Dizzy — none of it mattered. That night only the card game mattered, and Aunt Dizzy and I snapped our cards and laughed out loud as we changed suits, calling out aces, hearts, diamonds, spades, drinking our Coca-Colas and smelling like Cashmere Bouquet, the pink fairy on the motel sign blinking outside our room's picture window, my mother fast asleep beneath the pink counterpane.

I lay awake for a long time after Aunt Dizzy and I said our night-nights, and then after a while, I did something I hadn't done in years. I got out of my own bed and crawled in with my mother and Aunt Dizzy. My mother sighed and snuggled up against Aunt Dizzy to make room for me, as she had done so many nights before when I was little. I was so big now, I hardly fit.

Now and then a car drove by slowly on the highway, casting its fog-muffled lights across a small corner of the ceiling. When I awoke the next morning, my mother and Aunt Dizzy had already packed up the car, and we said goodbye to the Pink Motel. Out the rear window, I watched the neon fairy recede until she was no bigger than a charm. Then we turned onto the entrance ramp of the Blue Ridge Parkway, and she was gone for good, and we never spoke again of the night we slept in the Pink Motel or the day that led up to it.

THE NEXT YEAR I turned thirteen and my father was legally declared dead. My mother received a large sum of money from his life insurance policy and from the United States government, which financed, eventually, my college education — a degree in art history — and a used car — a well-maintained, low-mileage Karmann Ghia. During that year, too, the father of a friend of mine, Violet Nicco, was declared missing in action in Vietnam. A telegram from President Johnson had been delivered to Mrs. Nicco by a casualty officer. *We regret to inform you,* the letter began, and reading those words, Violet's mother fainted.

Only a few months after Violet's father disappeared, a more tangible tragedy shook the neighborhood. A boy not quite two years old who lived only a block away on the same street as ours — a dimpled, curly-haired little boy named Parker — crawled through a hedge and drowned in a goldfish pond in the next-door neighbor's yard. The child's mother was hanging up laundry, and in the time it took to hang a double-bed sheet, the child had disappeared, and by the time he was found, no more than ten minutes later, he was dead.

It was midsummer and every day the child's mother had brought the toddler, her youngest, out onto the lawn, where he played with clothespins on the grass or with a spoon and muffin tin in a wooden sandbox. Seeing the boy was nowhere in sight, the mother ran back into the house, thinking he'd taken off in that direction. His small body was found floating face-down like a cloth doll in the murky fish pond next door, the large, bright koi curious and distressed, flashing and darting about him — this big, pale intrusion in their dark waterworld.

By coincidence, little Parker's surname was Jones, the same as mine. Although tragedy had struck both families — Violet's and Parker's — during that summer of 1964, it was the Jones family, not Violet Nicco's, that received the lion's share of sympathy. The story of the drowned boy was in all the newspapers and on television stations across the state. It was the Jones family that received the flowers and prayer cards, the priest's visits, the tuna noodle casseroles and angel food cakes, while in Violet

Nicco's yard, the grass grew long and filled up with dandelions and dog dirt. Soggy newspapers accumulated along the wrought iron porch railing, and the flowerbeds, once full of marigolds and zinnias, reverted back to dandelion and ragweed.

Naturally, when the Jones boy drowned, there was some confusion in the community about which Jones family he belonged to, the surname being so common. When school commenced a few weeks after the drowning, I began ninth grade and entered the county's new consolidated high school six miles away. After homeroom the first day, the teacher stood by the door and touched my shoulder and asked in the kindest voice if it was my little brother who had drowned over the summer. I shook my head no. And in all but one of my classes on that first day, the teacher stopped me and asked the same thing — if I was the big sister of the little drowned boy — and each time then after homeroom, I crossed my fingers and averted my eyes and nodded yes.

I had cut out of the newspaper the photograph from the obituary of Parker Allan Jones, Jr., and soon after school started, I began to carry his picture in my wallet. The photo, underexposed and slightly out of focus, showed Parker in a checkered shirt and a cowboy hat, sitting in a highchair in front of a cake with two candles. One day in early October, I got up the courage during lunch period to show the picture to a new girl in my class, although my heart was pounding and I burst into tears before I could actually utter the terrible lie I had rehearsed. I was sent to the school nurse where I was given two Midol tablets and lay on a cot covered with a thin thermal blanket. I sobbed uncontrollably for twenty minutes and then was told to pull myself together, gather up my books, and return to class.

Just before Christmas the following year, Aunt Dizzy died from an influenza that had progressed to pneumonia, which her lungs could not resist, debilitated as they were from years of smoking unfiltered cigarettes. The gifts she had made for my mother and me sat under the Christmas tree well into February. I avoided the living room for weeks on end and spent most of my evenings in the kitchen, sitting at the Formica-top table, doing my homework, while my mother sat in the living room in the dark, with just the colored tree lights on.

One day around the end of February I came home from school to find that the tree and its ornaments were packed away. My mother and I opened our gifts from Aunt Dizzy that evening — a blue lamb's wool cardigan with a rolled collar for my mother and a striped muffler with matching mittens and cap with a pompom on top for me — and cried and cried, and then, for the first time in months, we watched *Jeopardy!,* Aunt Dizzy's favorite TV show.

My last years of high school passed without incident. In college I volunteered with Voices in Vital America, a nonprofit, nonpolitical student organization that distributed POW-MIA bracelets — simple, hand-hammered metal bands, each bearing the name of a soldier missing in action or taken prisoner of war in Southeast Asia. The bracelet was worn with the vow that it would not be removed until the soldier's status was known or he returned home. I was the first to sign up on our campus, and I returned to my room with the name Vincent Devron orbiting my wrist.

Long after I received his photograph and obituary three years later, I continued to wear the bracelet, never returning it to Vincent Devron's family like VIVA volunteers were supposed to do, and by the time I was in graduate school, Vincent Devron had become my childhood sweetheart, a handsome, curly-haired boy with dimples, a boy who wanted to join the circus but who ended up being drafted into the Army, a boy who juggled and had rigged up a tightrope in the backyard, a twelve-foot length of cable strung at shoulder height between two trees, which he practiced walking on with the aid of my umbrella. When I talked about Vincent Devron, I said he was still missing, and as I spoke of him, I lowered my voice, my eyes became moist, and I held on to the bracelet with his name on it like someone with palsy might hold their wrist to steady a glass or spoon.

I SEE NOW that I was always attracted to images, images imbued with meaning — POW-MIA bracelets and prayer cards, the obituary photograph of poor little Parker Jones. It's no wonder then that the profession I finally fell into — leading art tours — would involve immersing myself in images and expounding upon their attendant narratives and inspirations. I think the American search for meaning, which got into full swing by the sixties and continued up into the eighties with the New Age movement, was indicative of the times. It was the Cold War, after all, that strange period in American history full of tension and widespread fear: during air raid drills when we crawled under our desks and covered our heads — as if that could save us; during the Cuban Missile Crisis and the construction of the Berlin Wall; when race riots flared up in American cities; when the Kennedys and Martin Luther King, Jr., were assassinated, and the Manson Family committed the Tate-LaBianca murders; when the National Guard gunned down four students on the green grass of Kent State; when three Weathermen died in their West Village apartment as the bomb they were preparing and planning to detonate at an Army base in New Jersey accidentally exploded; when Patty Hearst was kidnapped and joined the Symbionese Liberation Army; and when death tolls from the "conflict overseas" scrolled across the bottom inch of television screens as casually as Mitch Miller lyrics.

Amidst all this mayhem and hysteria, Rod Serling's *The Twilight Zone* and *Night Gallery* captured the American imagination, and at one point, everyone was spinning a certain Beatles song backwards on their turntable, straining to hear the chant: *Paul is dead. Paul is dead.* It was around this time, the early seventies, that my mother became interested in — *obsessed with* is more accurate — the rapture and the prospect that we would all meet again as our best selves, in a better place. A few years after Aunt Dizzy died, my mother began to set aside things she might need, and before long the tiny bedroom in Ashport that had been mine, the room with the pink-and-white-striped wallpaper and the window overlooking the alley, was nothing more than a baggage claim for salvation, full of Woolworth's yarn and knitting needles, stacks of paperbacks and sweater patterns, canned goods, and jugs of water.

It seemed to me that my mother had confused the biblical Armageddon with a nuclear holocaust, understandably and maybe prophetically so, and that the heaven she envisioned was not much more than a gaudy fallout shelter with pearly gates, harps, and angels. Whether her preoccupation with the rapture was inspired by confusion over some government-issue preparedness brochure, a Jehovah's Witness tract, or perhaps a wager like Blaise Pascal's that she had arrived at on her own, I'll never know. One of the last things she had me do was drag down my father's old Fuller Brush case from the attic and position it in a corner of my old room, among all the other "necessities."

You just never know, Fanny, she said to me, shaking her head as she dusted the case carefully with an old pair of cotton underpants doused with Pledge. *You can never really know anything . . . You just go on with your life, Fanny, and you wonder. You wait. You wonder. You suppose.*

RECENTLY, I WATCHED a three-part television series about the earth sciences — geology, geography, cartography — and one of the scientists on the program said that in spite of the myriad of computerized geographic information systems we have at our fingertips today, you can never really know a place without ground-truthing it. That is, he said, walking it hectare by hectare to get a feel for the lay of the land, for the rise and fall of the earth under your feet; climbing its trees like Thoreau and look-ing out this way and that; wading, swimming, and paddling in its waters; flying over it low like a sparrow and high above like a Canada goose; knowing the call of the loon, the mating scream of the pileated woodpecker, the morning song of the common thrush, the scent of the night-blooming jasmine, the sticky abode of the caterpillar, the powdery trail of the moth.

In the social sciences and community medicine, I believe, there's a similar kind of truthing: the going into people's homes and observing their environment, listening to their stories, sit-ting at their kitchen tables, sampling their buttermilk biscuits, their homemade apple butter, their grandmother's secret recipe chow-chow.

For the human heart, though, how do you begin a truthing? I wanted to ask my mother back then as she dusted that big black Fuller Brush case — after all those years of silence — about the man we saw on that trip down into the Blue Ridge Mountains of North Carolina, that time we stayed in the Pink Motel. The man juggling Indian clubs and swallowing fire: was he the same man who carried me on his shoulders and chased me around the furniture in Zanesville, Ohio — the man who brought me Chiclets in slim yellow boxes and Cracker Jacks, too — the man who pretended to be an ogre and said he'd gobble me up? But asking that would have been, I suppose, like asking who was that little girl in pigtails, running about from room to room, squealing.

It was late, and I let the moment pass.

Acrophobia, i have heard it said, isn't a fear of heights at all or even a fear of falling as much as a desire to fall: the siren call of the void beckoning up to us to *give up, let go, fly!* It's a call we have all probably heard, at least for a split second, but few are brave enough, spontaneous enough, enamored, unmoored, or desperate enough to answer. Whoever that big man was at that carnival in North Carolina, I like to think now that he was my father, Walter Meriwether Jones. I want to believe that rather than that my father died perhaps a violent death along a wintry road or drowned in the icy Niagara. What I like best to believe is not that he deserted us but that he suffered at most a slight blow to the head — just a tap, really, like that made by a physician's rubber mallet testing a patient's reflexes — a tap that made my father forget forever my mother and me, and that he reinvented himself after that event, which my mother and I had done in many ways, too, and which I continue to do throughout my life, going from this thing to that.

The Christening

MIRIAM SAT DOWN and unbuttoned her blouse and leaned back against the monument, a life-size stone angel perched atop a huge granite plinth carved with garlands of laurel and twining morning glories. Above Miriam's head, deep cut in a beautiful scroll, the words *Patterson Family Grave* formed an arc, and in smaller block print was the inscription *For in that sleep of death what dreams may come when we have shuffled off this mortal coil?* After wandering up and down the maze of granite paths and hedgerows in the cemetery, Miriam finally settled on the angel, not for its grandeur or the inscription it bore or even for its family name or its plot — far away from the church — but for the angel's expression, which was either quizzical or worried, Miriam couldn't decide. The angel's eyebrows were slightly knitted, her head slightly cocked, and her lips a little pursed, as if someone had just whispered something to her that she didn't quite know how to take. A snide remark, perhaps, or an off-color joke.

What a relief it was to get outside that stuffy church, full of people fanning themselves with programs, and all the echoes, the wavering sopranos and resounding, magnified coughs bouncing off the stone walls like pinballs. And the sluggish pipe organ, which always seemed to be a fraction of a beat behind the voices. Oh, and *that woman!* That dreadful middle-aged woman beside her in the blue linen suit. How nervy she was, telling Miriam to hush when Miriam wasn't saying anything. Taking the hymnal out of Miriam's hands, clapping it shut, and replacing it in the pew in front of them before Miriam was even halfway through the Twenty-third Psalm.

"Thy rod and thy staff . . . ," Miriam said absently.

The woman in the blue linen suit had gone so far as to pass the collection plate right over Miriam and even pinch her upper arm and hiss at her to shush up as Miriam sang the doxology. Miriam should have sidled out of the pew and left right then, but she didn't want to make a scene, heels clicking on the stone floor, and she realized that the woman must be a little off, so to speak.

"There but for the grace of God . . . ," Miriam said, crossing herself and shaking her head.

The woman had been following Miriam for some time now, weeks or maybe even months. She often wore a disguise, sometimes a black knit turban or a short auburn wig, but Miriam was not fooled by any of this subterfuge. The woman had been driving the little red cab, in fact, that picked up Miriam this morning and brought her to the church. Miriam had hesitated before getting in, but the boy was sitting in the front seat, and Miriam knew the woman would not try to pull anything funny with the boy beside her. Miriam could trust the boy to look out for her.

"Bombs away," the boy said as Miriam climbed in and slammed the door, and the woman backed the cab out of the driveway and onto Little Indian Creek Road.

"Bombs away," Miriam replied.

✳   ✳   ✳

THE FIRST TIME Miriam had seen the woman was in her own home! Miriam was watching MTV and the woman walked right through the French doors like she owned the place. She set down a briefcase and a tapestry bag with wooden handles on the cobbler's bench, hung up a loden raincoat, and then paraded straight into Miriam's kitchen. She did it so brazenly that Miriam was more dumbfounded than startled. It was raining, a slow steady drizzle, and outside the French doors the peonies were in full bloom, their soggy white blossoms drooping on the flagstones like wads of Kleenex. For a split second, Miriam even considered the possibility that she had imagined the whole thing: the woman, the bag, the briefcase, the raincoat. Very quietly, she got up from the couch and tiptoed from the living room into the hall. There was the bag. There was the briefcase. There was the damp coat. Miriam peeped around the kitchen corner. There was the strange woman filling up Miriam's copper teakettle from Miriam's tap!

"What on earth!" Miriam said to herself, appalled by the intruder's audacity, and backed away from the doorway, tiptoeing backwards to the stairway, then turning and climbing the stairs. On the landing, Miriam paused and listened. The boy was just starting down the stairs, and Miriam put one finger to her lips and with her other hand motioned him to stop.

"Shhhh," Miriam cautioned. She picked up the phone in the landing and pressed zero. "Police," she whispered into the receiver. "Get me the police right away. A strange woman is making tea in my kitchen!"

"Way to go, Marple," the boy cheered, giving Miriam a high-five. He leaned closer, smelling of pungent tobacco and Listerine. "Listen, whatever you do," he warned her, "don't drink the tea. It's laced with LSD."

"OK," Miriam whispered and smiled at the boy, "but who is she?"

"Her name is Commando Leary," the boy whispered in her ear. Miriam could feel his tiny gold nose ring brush against her cheek. "She was sent here by the Central Grammarian Elizabethan Tramalfagorian Liberation Army to monitor our behavior and alter our brain waves. She operates on us while we sleep. The cat — Rosencrantz — is her surgeon general."

"No!" Miriam inhaled, bringing her hands to her face. "You can't mean it?"

The boy was wearing what he wore most days: a black T-shirt with a Day-Glo green drawing of an alien — or maybe it was an insect — with outsized, slanted white eyes. WE ARE HERE TO HELP YOU the T-shirt said. One holiday, the boy had given Miriam the exact same shirt, wrapped in tinfoil.

"But as long as you don't drink the tea, you're safe. Just don't drink the tea. She can't operate on us if we don't drink the tea. Got it? Don't drink the tea. Don't drink the tea. It's laced with LSD."

Miriam nodded and picked up the chant. "Don't drink the tea! It's laced with LSD!"

"Don't drink the tea!" With his index fingers, the boy beat out the rhythm on the banister.

"OK, let's go." In mock gallantry, the boy took Miriam by the arm and began singing a jazzy, syncopated version of "The Wedding March" as they descended the stairs.

"Here comes the bride," he sang in a Louis Armstrong rasp, snapping his fingers, "all step aside."

"Don't drink the tea," Miriam belted out. "It makes you pee."

But the police never came that day, and the woman in Miriam's house began to appear more and more frequently. Sometimes she came and sat right beside Miriam in the front room, carrying that same tapestry bag, which contained balls of fuzzy, heather blue yarn and shiny aluminum knitting needles. *Tic-tic-*

tic went the needles when the woman knitted. Miriam moved from the couch to the recliner, straightening an antimacassar on the way. Even though she preferred her own corner of the couch, Miriam wanted to keep an eye on the woman and her pointy needles, which possibly doubled as operating instruments. Miriam reported any and all suspicious moves of Commando Leary to the boy, who logged them in invisible ink — for security reasons, he said — into a small black address book he kept in his back pocket.

"How can you watch that stuff?" the strange woman would say and flip the television channel to people talking, without even asking Miriam's permission. Miriam watched only MTV. Often the boy would join her, and sometimes a waifish-looking girl named Tess, with a flat chest and stringy hair. Tess had tiny gold earrings all up and down her earlobes and one in her nose — like the boy's. Tess sometimes wore the tiniest black T-shirt — sized for a baby, Miriam thought — that announced, MY INNER CHILD HAS A NOSE RING, and underneath the T-shirt her tiny nipples stood out like Hershey's kisses.

To prevent Commando Leary from changing the channels, Miriam had to hide the remote control. Sometimes she slipped it in between the cushions of the couch, but usually the woman found it there, so Miriam began concealing the remote control in her bra, or in a brown paper Giant Eagle bag she kept by her side and carried with her wherever she went.

After a while, though, the woman quit coming into the front room and spent more and more time lying on the day bed in the den, with the venetian blinds closed. She lay with her back to the wall, the door ajar, an afghan thrown over her bare legs. Miriam walked by many times and sometimes just stood in the doorway, but the woman never moved. Once Miriam entered the room and picked up the afghan, which had slid onto the floor, and

covered the woman's legs. The woman didn't move, but Miriam
could tell she wasn't sleeping.

"Boo!" Miriam whispered.

OH, THE BABY, the dear little infant next to Miriam in church
was so sweet — not more than two or three months old — and
the little girl, too, and so well behaved, Miriam mused as she
leaned against the stone angel. They reminded Miriam of her
own babies, Celeste and Pauli. They had those same tight curls,
nappy curls like little Negro babies, like their father. "Pickaninnies," Miriam's mother called the little Negro babies when
they rode the trolley downtown. Miriam was just a little girl
then and her mother so prim and proper in her wide-brim hat
with the tickly ostrich feather, but now *pickaninnies* was an ugly
word.

"Pickaninnies," Miriam whispered shamefully, clicking her
tongue and shaking her head.

How Miriam loved to bury her face in Celeste's and Pauli's
hair, drawing them to her and kissing their heads, their soft
dark curls, the clean almond scent of baby powder and baby
soap and sunshine. "My little lambs," she'd coo into their curls.

"My sweet little Persian lambs," Miriam said dreamily, her
eyes moist with tears, "where are you now?"

Miriam opened her purse and took out her compact, small
and octagonal and inlaid with mother-of-pearl. "What a lovely
gift a compact is," Miriam said to herself. Every time she opened
it she saw Russell in his uniform the day he gave it to her. It was
the first gift he'd ever given her, and she'd kept it all these years,
opening and closing it every day with its precise, reassuring
click. The tiny engraving on the bottom had said TO MIRIAM,
LOVE RUSSELL, but it was so worn that only the word TO and the
last four letters of RUSSELL were still discernible: TO SELL it said.
In between and all around that phrase was a blackish-greenish

thumbprint where the gold plating had worn off and the tarnished brass showed through.

"To sell," Miriam said.

She dabbed at the moist area around her eyes and drew the powder puff across the bridge of her nose, then winked in the mirror and snapped the compact shut. She smoothed her pleated skirt and slipped off her shoes. A good pair of beige pumps with a sensible heel is always a sound investment, Miriam reminded herself, admiring her shoes. As long as you keep your hose in the beige and blush hues, even ivories, and don't venture into the taupes and grays, you could wear a good pair of beige pumps with anything.

"Beige pumps, yessirree," Miriam said, pleased with her shoes and with herself for making such a wise purchase.

The sky, the sky here is so big. So big and full of clouds, and the land is so flat and everything so neat and organized. Miriam felt as if she were sitting on an empty cake platter, painted with a Currier and Ives scene and covered with a glass dome. She breathed deeply and began to relax, the carved angel with folded wings towering above her. The whole church experience had been quite upsetting. That poor woman, Miriam thought, that poor woman in the blue linen suit whom Miriam had had the misfortune of sitting next to. Thank God she was able to push through the congregation after the service and slip out the side door the choir used. What if the woman had followed her?

"Just think!" Miriam said, shaking her head.

What a beautiful day. Clear and warm and breezy and the sky so full of clouds. "A perfect day for Michelangelo," Miriam remarked.

She removed her blouse and folded it neatly around her pocketbook to make a pillow, complete with pillowcase, and lay down on her back, the TV's remote control strapped to her sternum by her crisscross bra. Miriam was good at Michelangelo. It was a game her sister Gracie had taught her. Miriam, in turn, had taught her own children, Celeste and Pauli, and even her husband, Russell, although Russell wasn't very good at it. Where were Celeste and Pauli now? Miriam wondered. And Russell? When was the last time she'd seen them?

"Clouds, clouds, paint some pictures for me, what will they be? Roll over, Michelangelo, and make room for me!" Miriam recited and closed her eyes. She counted to ten, rolled over one full turn, opened her eyes, and began to name the cloud pictures above her. In Michelangelo, you had to name each cloud picture and its position, and if you stopped for more than the count of ten, it was the next person's turn.

"Chicken," she said. "Chicken in the middle. Chicken in a tuxedo with a soup spoon and a suitcase!

"Two monkeys," she called, pointing. "Two monkeys to the right. Two little monkeys doing the Charleston!

"Toaster! Toaster to the left!" Miriam continued, pulling the remote control from her bra, pointing it at the sky, and kicking off her shoes. "Toaster on a pedestal!

"Man in a bow tie two clouds over. Man with glasses and a sombrero and a bow tie. President Truman. President Harry S. Truman. President Harry S. Truman in a sombrero . . . playing a glockenspiel!"

Miriam flung the remote control into the air and cupped her hands around her mouth. "Give 'em hell! Give 'em hell, Harry," she shouted into the magnificent, animated canopy of sky as Harry Truman's nose began to dissolve and Carmen Miranda on a Harley-Davidson floated by.

"WHAT A PIECE of work is a man!" a voice above Miriam boomed.

Miriam opened her eyes and looked up.

"How noble in reason! How infinite in faculty! How like an angel!" There was the boy in his alien T-shirt standing atop the monument with one arm draped around the angel's shoulder, the other arm extended, hand wagging Miriam's remote control in the sky.

With an exaggerated gesture — eyes rolling, tongue protruding — he pretended to study the remote control and finally pressed a button. "And now, for a real toe-tappin' good time," the boy said in a thick Hungarian accent, "we bring you the lovely little Lennon Sisters with 'Tie a Yellow Ribbon.'" He batted at imaginary bubbles around the angel's face and pressed another button on the remote. Strumming a low-slung air guitar, he broke into "Lady Madonna," then stopped abruptly after the first few bars.

"Say, bloke, do your feet stink?" he looked down and asked Miriam, quite seriously, in a cockney accent. "Does your heart ache? Suffer no more, bloke. Try Dr. Pedi-Coeur's Hoof n' Heart Powder! It stings a little . . . but . . . hey . . . whatever!"

"Geronimo!" he yelled and leapt down. "Get dressed, Marple. The Commando is on your track and she's having a hissy fit. The christening's over. Everybody's headed out, and the Commando is, well, let's just say 'livid.' And livid does not become her. Frankly, you didn't miss anything."

Miriam put on her blouse and the boy extended his hand.

Miriam drew back. "I fear thee, ancient mariner," she protested with a dramatic shudder. "I fear thy skinny hand!"

Together they headed for the little red taxi waiting at the cemetery gate.

CELESTE WAITED IN the car while Julian went to fetch his grandmother. It wasn't the first time she'd wandered off. Miriam never went far, but sometimes she hid like a little child and giggled when they found her. Celeste looked around, and finding the few remaining cars in the church parking lot empty, she took off her wig and scratched her head, then put it back on and straightened it in the rearview mirror. Maybe she should forgo the hot, stretchy wig and just shave her head, get it tattooed! and a nose ring! and wear a hundred tiny gold rings in her ears like Tess. It was not vanity that made her wear the wig, that was certain. It was just that she didn't want Julian to see her bald. She wanted to keep him from confronting the inevitable devastation of the flesh. She wanted to spare him. And, too, she secretly hoped that by not giving in to the appearance of disease she was actually fooling it, staving it off.

Today was the last day of rest. Tomorrow began not just the second session of summer school but another round of treatment. Celeste felt sick just thinking about it. And today, when she would like more than anything to be alone, to rest, to pull herself together, to maybe sink into the cool darkness of a Sunday matinee, her sister-in-law had planned the baby's christening, and of course, Celeste would have to take Miriam. She recited her standard daily prayer, "Please, just get me through today," she mouthed to the eyes of the tired stranger in the rearview mirror, then turned away before the stranger could reply.

"This is wonderful bread. Did you bake it yourself?" Miriam asked for the tenth time in as many minutes. She held the thick slice of bread to her nose and breathed in its delicious aroma. Above the crust, Miriam peeped out demurely and smiled at the maitre d', a woman with frosted hair who sat across from her at the banquet table, which stretched from one end of the stone patio to the next. Two umbrellas shaded the table, and under one, a baby in a carrier slept, surrounded by packages wrapped in colored paper and tied with shiny bows.

But before the maitre d' could answer, the woman in the blue linen suit — yes, she had followed Miriam to the country club! — piped up in her irritating tone, "No. Mother. For the third time, I bought the bread at Giant Eagle!" The edge in her voice was as sharp as the steak knife on her plate, and Miriam felt the familiar wave of tears welling up behind her breastbone in the place she thought of as the tear pond, behind the remote control.

If she could touch the remote control, she could, perhaps — like the boy — flip the channel.

"Don't call me your mother!" Miriam snapped, blinking back tears. A long silence ensued, and Miriam looked across the table for some reassurance, some kind word from the maitre d', but the woman with the frosted hair was staring at her plate, engrossed in navigating a tiny piece of lettuce around with her fork.

"So . . . Celeste," a man to Miriam's right began rather loudly, "when is Julian off to England with the drama club?"

"Say, bloke," Miriam announced gaily, "do your feet stink? Does your heart ache?" Miriam sniffled and looked up at the sky. A cloud chariot was approaching from the right, the driver brandishing a whip.

"And who is this new drama teacher now who's taking them? Wasn't he in a play on Broadway or something?" the loud man continued, ignoring Miriam's commercial.

"Charlton Heston," Miriam remarked.

The loud man burst out laughing, and a stout woman with a long gray braid pushed back her chair and began hastily, noisily, to gather up the china plates. Other people rose immediately from the table, as if on cue, clattering silverware and glasses, scraping meat scraps onto one plate while a big black dog sat nearby, drooling and smiling. A great commotion rose up. A great urgency to clear the table, leaving Miriam and the loud man seated at one end, the baby at the other, while people scurried in and out of the glass doors, carrying dishes, condiments, bowls. Only the bread basket remained. Miriam reached for the next-to-last slice of bread.

"This is wonderful bread. Did you bake it yourself?" Miriam smiled and questioned the loud man in her sweetest voice.

The loud man looked away.

The woman in the blue linen suit, who had just set down a stack of dessert plates, put her head in her hands and sighed.

"Shoot me. Just shoot me," she said, and tossed a tea towel in the air.

"Bam-bam-bam!" said the boy, who appeared from nowhere, sticking his finger in the back of the woman who wished to be shot.

"Marple," the boy said, turning to Miriam, "report to headquarters immediately."

"Julian, don't," the woman in the blue suit pleaded. "Please don't, don't get her going. It's bad enough —" Celeste stopped in midsentence and wiped her forehead with the back of her hand.

"Chill out, Mom," Julian said, and began to tickle his mother, unknowingly touching the tiny lump under her arm, which her clothes and skin and heart concealed.

Miriam saluted, and the boy pulled up a chair beside her.

"Alas, how is it with you, lady, that you with the incorporeal air do hold discourse?" The boy leaned on his elbow and winked at Miriam, with the other hand motioning his mother away. "The one who bore me . . . the one whom you bore, the boarish boor you bore who bores me (forgive me, Mother!) . . . she means thee no harm." Miriam smiled and blinked. "She suffers from a foul ailment of the flesh that has left her disfigured and its potion has mortified her roots. But, hark, what treachery lurks in the molded plastic chairs of Lord Walton that grace this great hall? The bread, I tell you, *is* homemade, Maid Miriam, 'tis not from Giant Eagle, and thou hast been, milady, deceived."

Miriam pulled the bread basket toward her and casually dumped the contents — one small slice, two heels, and a multitude of crumbs — into her purse.

CELESTE AWOKE IN a sweat, rolled over on the day bed, and looked at the clock. Two twenty-two A.M. Today was the dreaded Monday. A prescription and a glass of stale water sat on the maple desk, illuminated by the clock's glow. Celeste sighed and slid her hand to the now familiar lump that had grown in her armpit — overnight it seemed — like a pearl. "Whether 'tis nobler in the mind to suffer the slings and arrows of outrageous fortune or to take arms against a sea of troubles . . . a sea of troubles . . . a pearl in a sea of troubles," Celeste repeated. "To say we end the heartache and the thousand natural shocks the flesh is heir to . . . heir to."

Could she endure another surgery and more chemo and radiation, and for what? For Julian? For Miriam? Where else in these mortal coils did the cancer cells spin? What would she do when Julian was gone . . . without him to babysit Miriam? What would he do without her? But in no time, he'd be gone for good. He'd graduate from high school next spring, his life glimmering before him like a lantern. Beckoning. A neon lighthouse. How could she juggle the teaching, the eldercare, the treatment? She could cut back to part-time, but what about insurance? The prescription drugs? Maybe Paul could take Mother. No. Paul was no help at all. Would Celeste have to send her own mother away now — from her own home? In what cerebral hinterland did Miriam already dwell?

A tempestuous storm had danced across the northeast most of the night, waltzing its way to a salty rendezvous with the eastern shore. Now, in the still interval between night and day, just the scent of rain remained, a wilting orchid on the voile wrap of dawn. In the suburban silence, Celeste lay awake, weary, lonely, longing, listening. The thin, high-pitched buzz of a transformer, the octaves lower drone of a billion insects genuflecting in the wet lawn. Far away, a siren's scream. Amidst the dull electric-invertebrate hum, Celeste listened with her whole body. She could almost hear the caterpillars dropping from the cherry trees outside her window. The porch light was still on. Where was Julian? Why wasn't he home yet, and what was he doing? Celeste worried, but the white silence would not yield, would not give her what she strained to hear: the shlish of tires in the wet driveway, Julian's key turning in the lock, his footsteps on the stairs.

Then inside the house . . . a creak . . . a stirring . . . the familiar plastic-on-parquet scuffing sound of her mother shuffling down the hall in her threadbare bunny slippers. Miriam paused in the doorway of the den. Celeste held her breath and closed her eyes, feigning sleep. Through a frayed fringe of eyelashes, Celeste watched the gigantic Day-Glo eyes on her mother's black T-shirt approach the day bed, Miriam's frizzy hair a blue fluorescent halo illuminated by the stripes of blue streetlight slicing through the venetian blinds.

Miriam laid a gnawed remnant of bread crust on the desk, then gathered up the crumpled afghan and shook it, once, twice, and placed it gently over Celeste, drawing it up to her shoulders, tucking her in. She laid her hands on Celeste's bald, powdered head and, bending over, kissed the crown. A sea of crumbs fell like brittle stars on Celeste's closed eyes.

"My poor little lamb," Miriam muttered. "My poor little Persian lamb."

Reading Raymond Carver,
Waiting for Bob Dylan

IT WAS THE MIDDLE of the night, and we were on a train in Morocco, four, maybe five thousand miles from home, en route from Marrakesh to Casablanca, heading home from a trip that had begun in southern Spain. The vacation was over, and the arduous journey back to the United States had begun: this train to Casablanca, another train to Tangier, then the ferry to Algeciras, bus to Sevilla, bullet train from Sevilla to Madrid, metro to the airport, then the transatlantic flight to Newark, another flight to Dulles International, shuttle to Park & Fly, another three hours driving home. Everything connected by intricate timetables printed on cheap paper, carved in stone.

To make Monday morning's flight, we must catch tomorrow's ferry. To make that ferry, we must catch this train. To catch this train, we must . . .

What had happened was, we'd missed the five P.M. train from Marrakesh to Casablanca. The next train left at midnight.

When we bought our tickets that afternoon, the man in

the ticket booth had told us quite plainly in French that the train to Casablanca would depart at six P.M. Stupidly, we hadn't double-checked the schedule, which we found baffling and hard to read. We arrived at five P.M., just to be safe — and early —just as the train to Casablanca was blowing her horn and ringing her bell, leaving the station. Now we had no more dirhams, the banks were closed, and the ticket officer would not change our tickets.

While Phillip stood at the ticket window, trying to explain in French — which neither of us spoke well — our predicament to a Moroccan ticket agent who understood only bits and pieces of his country's second language, two young men pressed against me until I found myself backed against a wall. They taunted me for money and cigarettes, of which I had neither. I tried to explain. A small, beautiful boy, no older than five or six, joined in, sticking his skinny arm and hand — no bigger than a plastic back scratcher — down my jacket pocket, and with the other hand yanking at my purse, all the while grinning and flashing a set of perfect, dazzling white teeth.

Just moments before there had been an altercation between some young men in black watch caps and black leather jackets. A knife blade flashed. Two policemen appeared out of nowhere with automatic weapons. With his back to the excitement, Phillip stood irate at the ticket window, bending down and yelling through the small chest-high hole in the window.

"*L'homme a dit six heures!*" he shouted above the thunder of the station.

"*Quel homme, Ali Baba?*" the man in the ticket booth shouted back, throwing up his arms, which flashed perspiration stains like black holes.

The line of annoyed travelers behind Phillip lengthened as departure time to other cities approached. I found an empty seat near a door leading to the boarding platform and dragged our bags over to it, stuffing one bag under the seat, holding one on my lap, another planted firmly under my feet, the webbed strap wrapped around my ankle.

Many minutes passed as Phillip and the ticket man argued in English-French-Arabic and hand signs, shouting and waving tickets and pointing at the clock. Then an armed official-looking man in a stiff uniform and pompous cap arrived and took Phillip by the arm, unlocked a metal fire door, and led him through it. Phillip turned to me and raised his hands to his face, shrugging his shoulders and miming Munch's *Scream* before the door slammed shut. I dug in the bag under my feet and pulled out my Raymond Carver.

I looked around the terminal, then stuck my nose into my book, *Where I'm Calling From,* the big Vintage Contemporaries collection of Carver's stories. Phillip, who loves to travel and has been to Africa a number of times, brought *Justine* and *Balthazar* from the *Alexandria Quartet* for reading material. I brought the latest *New Yorker* and Raymond Carver because I wanted to stay home but had somehow, at Phillip's insistence, agreed to accompany him on this trip. And so I sat and sat, guardian of our bags, reading Raymond Carver, the Marion Ettlinger photograph of him on the cover staring out point-blank, staring out like a big cougar.

In the Marrakesh souks I'd bought as souvenirs seventeen sterling silver hands of Fatima, which were now stuffed in my suitcase. Like horseshoes in America and trumpeting elephants in India, the hand of Fatima appears above Muslim doorways, portending good fortune and staving off the evil eye — a talisman for protection.

Seventeen hands, I kept whispering to myself as reassurance while I sat there reading Raymond Carver. *Seventeen hands of Fatima. Seventeen hands of Fatima. Seventeen . . .* I kept looking toward the steel door, but Phillip was nowhere in sight. Only after "Chef's House" and "So Much Water So Close to Home" would he reappear, smiling, waving tickets, shuffling toward me in his loose sandals. We would be on the next train, which would depart in five and a half hours.

BY THE TIME we boarded the train, we were both exhausted, and Phillip fell asleep almost as soon as the Marrakesh Express left the station. I, ever the insomniac, knew I was in for the long haul; I'd be awake until we arrived in Casablanca around five A.M. Phillip slept curled on the seat, with his head on my lap, my pashmina shawl over him, as we passed through the desert, mile after mile of utter darkness and emptiness, heading for the coast. Here and there, a cluster of lights glimmered for a moment like will-o'-the-wisp and then was gone just as quickly as it had appeared, and each time I looked up from my book and out the window, I was startled by my own reflection: a bedraggled, middle-aged woman with messy hair, a face looking older in the dim greenish light, a face grown flat as a dime. Sometimes through that strange reflection, I thought I saw camels and tents and caravans; I thought I heard music, bells, and dancers' bangles. I thought I heard Maria Muldaur singing "Midnight at the Oasis." Oh, god, I was tired.

After an hour or so, Phillip's head felt like a cinderblock, and my right leg was numb. By the time the train reached the port city of El Jadida and began to stitch its way along the hem of the African coast, we'd been on it for nearly four hours, and I'd read nearly all of *Where I'm Calling From.* All my old favorites: "Cathedral," and "What We Talk About When We Talk About Love," "Feathers," "Where I'm Calling From," "Menudo."

I relaxed and made myself as comfortable as possible. The stories were getting better. There were ones I'd never read before: "Elephant," "Whoever Was Using This Bed," "Blackbird Pie." I pushed the button on my indiglo Timex. Three fifty-three. I had reached the last story: "Errand."

"Chekhov," the story begins. Just that name, that word. "On the evening of March 27, 1897, he went to dinner in Moscow . . ."

I HAD READ "Errand" before, about ten years earlier in a night class in American short fiction. There were some bad things going on in my life then, and I took the class to help boost my self-esteem and to get me out of the funk I was in. My friend Hollis talked me into signing up.

I don't know what was the matter with me back then when I was taking a class with Hollis and reading Raymond Carver, whether it was something in particular or just some great general depression — which I was prone to — but whatever, the first time I read "Errand" it made me so sad. I knew it was the last story Raymond Carver had ever published and that he probably knew he had lung cancer when he wrote it, just like Chekhov knew for years that he was dying from tuberculosis, and I could just feel the death in "Errand" — Carver's own death — as the momentum moving the story of Chekhov's final hours forward in a quiet, processional way. I could feel Carver writing it. Like the blind man's hand in "Cathedral" riding the hand of the narrator as he draws on the grocery store bag — the arches, the windows, the flying buttresses, the doors — here was Carver's own death riding piggyback on his story about the death of Anton Chekhovs.

When I got to the part where Chekhov takes his last drink — a sip of champagne ordered by the attending physician, who knows that a doctor is now superfluous, that death is present in the room too, waiting like a porter to claim the great writer — and Chekhov says, "It's been so long since I tasted champagne," I could feel Carver's alcohol addiction crying out, the dark other hunkered down inside his body like a figure out of one of the Black Goyas, which Phillip and I had seen at the Prado in Madrid, like a violent, half-witted family member locked in the fruit cellar, making its own death wish now before leaving, a hoarse whisper from the back of the throat. How long had it been then since Carver had sworn off drink? Ten years? More? Why not have a drink now, Raymond Carver, like Chekhov — a last toast to your life, your magnificent gift — now that Death has made his presence, his errand, known?

After Anton Chekhov died — late on a sultry summer night in 1904 — his widow, the actress Olga Knipper, sat by her husband's body in the hotel in Badenweiler, a spa and resort city in the Black Forest where Chekhov had gone to die. Olga sat until dawn next to her beloved's body, next to the small tabouret with the three half-empty champagne glasses. She sat there, in Carver's words, "until daybreak, when thrushes began to call from the garden below. Then came the sound of tables and chairs being moved about." Carver quotes from Olga Knipper's journal, July 2, 1904, the night of her vigil: "There were no human voices, no everyday sounds. There was only beauty, peace, and the grandeur of death."

The grandeur of death.

When i first read "Errand," I was living on Market Street in Indian Creek, in a small brick house with plaster walls and hardwood floors. It was a Sears mail-order house from around 1905. When I lived alone with my dog in that house and read "Errand," I knew that in the same situation, were I Olga Knipper, I wouldn't have let those three half-finished glasses of champagne just sit there; I'd have finished them off and whatever else was left in the bottle, too. And I reckoned that probably Raymond Carver would have done the same.

I had an audiotape then that my friend Dean had given me for Christmas a few years earlier. *Songs of Eastern Song Birds* it was called. It came with a stapled booklet with colored pictures of birds, and beside each bird was a number that corresponded to the footage on the tape where that bird's song was recorded. Underneath each bird was a short description of it, its range and

habitat, its flight patterns, the rapidity of its wing beats, its manners (e.g., shy, inquisitive, raucous), and the variations between
the sexes (e.g., female muted). After I finished reading "Errand," I got out the tape and listened to the song of the common
thrush.

"Ee-o-lay," it sang. "Ee-o-lay." And then a man's voice said,
"Thrush."

"Ee-o-lay, ee-o-lay," went the thrush again, then a rapid "pip-
pip-pip-pip."

"Thrush," the man said again.

Then it was silent.

I got into the habit of coming home from work and pouring
myself a drink and then listening to the voices of that thrush and
of the man on the tape, then turning off the tape player and
moving a chair away from the little table in my dining room.
Listening. The chair made that scraping sound on the oak floor,
the sound that Olga Knipper must have heard beneath her in
that stirring hotel in the Black Forest. My house on Market
Street was old, and the glass in the dining room windows was
wavy and distorted and beautiful. Outside those windows was a
little slate patio and a stone wall and beyond the wall an empty
lot overgrown with stinging nettle, thistle, and ironweed, and a
couple of joe-pyes taller than me. Planted along the wall were
some old-fashioned bushes: a big, foamy spirea, a mock orange, a dark lilac, a scribble of forsythia, and a yellow rose that
climbed the wall, then flung itself over it like a convict in a
chintz jumpsuit, making a great, if conspicuous escape. Two
holly trees on the corner — a male and female — blocked the
street from view.

By that time in my life, I already knew a lot of dead people.
After I listened to the birdsong and the little chairsong, I would
stand in the silence behind that sinuous glass and sip my drink
and look out the window at those old things and cry for all the
people I'd known who were now gone forever from Earth and

for Anton Pavlovich Chekhov and Raymond Clevie Carver. Then I would lie down on the couch and usually fall asleep for a bit. When I woke up, my dog, Figaro, would be sitting there, staring at me, waiting to go for his walk. His mouth would be slightly open, his pink tongue peeking out from his brown muzzle like a piece of bologna from the edge of a pumpernickel roll. I would get up and splash some water on my face, have another quick drink, and then walk with Figgy around the neighborhood, looking in the lighted windows of the neighborhood houses and the mom-and-pop stores.

A block away on Arch was Baker's corner grocery and Goodwin's Pharmacy a few doors down, and behind Arch ran the long alley people called Dog Alley. In the window of Goodwin's, a gangly old geranium grew with two long gnarled branches that forked out from the middle of a terra cotta pot, making it look like a divining rod amidst the display of Ace bandages and Rid Lice shampoo. In the back of the store, a few steps up from the greeting cards and the single aisle of Tylenol, Preparation H, and Pine Brothers cough drops, old Mr. Goodwin sat every day behind the counter in his white coat. For fortysome years, Mr. Goodwin and his wife, Naomi, had lived in a tiny apartment above the store. Naomi had a long narrow face with a purple birthmark shaped like Florida on one cheek. She wore bright red lipstick and worked the cash register. After she died, Mr. Goodwin rented the apartment to university students and lived in the storage room in the back of the store, separated from the pharmacy by a flowered curtain, green with sprigs of white dogwood. At night a single fluorescent light and the dim blue glow leaking from a television in the back room illuminated the pharmacy like a weird terrarium.

A grassy median ran down the middle of Arch Street from Goodwin's Pharmacy to Gene's Beer Garden, and in this strip all the neighborhood dogs did their business. I walked in the street, and Figgy walked in cautious circles around the trees, sniffing and peeing. One newer, ranch-style house on the corner of Morris and Arch had a rec room with a picture window, the curtains never drawn. Spotlighted on the back wall were mounted heads of wild animals — a zebra, a tiger, a bear, a moose — all lined up as if they were standing on boxes on the other side of the knotty pine paneling, their heads poking through, posing for some great white hunter theme park snapshot. In another house two blocks away, a grander house on Park, a harp stood on display in front of a picture window, and sometimes when Figgy and I walked by, a lady with her hair pulled back into a tight bun would be playing the harp, working the pedals and plucking the strings with great show, reaching and plucking, reaching and plucking, the harp leaning on her shoulder, her elbows flapping up and out like wings, but from the sidewalk you couldn't hear a sound.

Sometimes on these dog walks I'd pass the whistler. He was a stout, elderly man — I believe his name was Felix — who was stooped over and walked with his hands clasped behind his back. The whistler was short, his body almost square, his waist as wide as Humpty Dumpty's. Because he walked all stooped over, he seemed even shorter than he was, no taller, say, than the back of a kitchen chair. Sometimes in the daytime I'd see the whistler at Murphy's lunch counter, slurping a bowl of chili or ham and bean soup, his face nearly in the bowl. He wore a Pittsburgh Pirates baseball cap and walked so bent over that you couldn't see his face, and while he walked he whistled different bird calls very loudly, often at the pretty high school girls who crossed the bridge every day into our neighborhood, going to and from the Catholic school.

A LONG TIME ago, I knew another whistler. His name was Jay Johnson. This was back when I was in high school and we lived out off the Little Indian Creek Road. I haven't been back there in years, but I hear it's totally built up now with housing developments and gated communities. Back in the sixties, though, there was still a lot of farmland, and the developments like the one we lived in were novel. On Sundays, people from all around Cook County drove out to the developments to tour the model homes and marvel at their shag carpets, sliding glass doors, and built-in wall ovens. About two miles from our house, down a long hill, was a big, secluded mental hospital where Woody Guthrie spent his last years. People who worked there said that Woody Guthrie's son, Arlo, accompanied by his friend Bob Dylan, used to come out there from New York City to see Woody.

Back then, my best friend, Bobbie, and I were crazy about Bob Dylan, and we'd both read Woody Guthrie's book *Bound for Glory*. The summer we were fifteen, Bobbie and I used to walk down to the asylum every day in our ironed sleeveless blouses, madras shorts, and buffalo hide sandals. We'd sit on the fieldstone wall that surrounded the hospital, smoking cigarettes, hoping to see Arlo Guthrie and Bob Dylan. We'd sit there on the wall, swinging our legs and singing "Blowin' in the Wind" and "Don't Think Twice, It's All Right" and "Song to Woody."

We never saw Bob Dylan or Woody or Arlo Guthrie, but we saw mental patients sometimes, a single-file parade of them in their loose, pastel gowns, walking from one building to another like zombies, and once there was a great deal of thrashing in a car entering the gate, and we heard a woman screaming.

One day Bobbie and I walked from the mental institution to the Barn Door restaurant about another two miles away, at the intersection of Route 22 and Little Indian Creek Road. We went there to buy cigarettes because there was a machine in the foyer, and you didn't have to go up to a counter and ask for them. At the Barn Door we bought a pack of Parliaments for thirty-five cents and ordered two Coca-Colas. We sat at the counter, acting grownup, smoking our cigarettes and sipping our sodas, spinning this way and that on our stools, gossiping about boys we knew, talking about Bob Dylan, and in the mirror behind the counter stacked with trays of glasses and stainless steel ice cream dishes, I saw my father's two-tone Chrysler pull up. My father got out and went around to the passenger side and opened the door. Out stepped our neighbor Mrs. Alberghetti in tight brown capri pants, a brown sleeveless shell, and black cat's-eye sunglasses. Her dyed-black hair was teased and piled up on top of her head, and she carried a floppy purse decorated with large pieces of tropical fruit.

Mrs. Alberghetti bred toy poodles and lived on Mari-Kay Lane in a brick rancher a few houses down from Bobbie. One summer, not long after we'd moved to Indian Creek, my father took my cousin Trudy and me over to Mrs. Alberghetti's to see a litter of toy poodles. We cuddled them and let them bite us with their tiny needle teeth while their mother barked at us from behind a gate. Then we went upstairs to the kitchen where Mrs. Alberghetti served us lemonade made with tap water, sugar, and Real Lemon. She had a thick German accent. "Do you vont zum lemonade?" Rosa Alberghetti asked us, and we tried not to giggle. It tasted like warm water with a dash of Lysol, and Trudy spit it back into the metal glass.

My father touched Mrs. Alberghetti's elbow as he slammed the car door, and I watched in the mirror as he held the restaurant door for her and the hostess seated them in one of the booths in the dining room and handed them the Mother Goose–size menus. A few weeks later, my father brought home a toy poodle pup that my mother named Charles de Gaulle.

OUR HOUSE WAS off of Little Indian Creek Road, the main road, which was fronted mostly by old farms and fieldstone houses close to the road, with maybe a snowball bush by the front porch and a pine tree nearby; a small apple orchard off to one side; an old, ramshackle barn and a cow pond clogged with reeds and cattail, along its bank a row of orange daylilies and a long weathered-gray bench.

The tracts of houses like the ones where Bobbie's family and mine lived were built in the sixties and seventies and often had streets named after the developers' daughters. Ours was called Cher-Lee Circle, and Bobbie lived on Mari-Kay Lane. Jay Johnson lived in the old Johnson homestead, the original farmhouse on Little Indian Creek Road, and he walked all night through the streets of the new developments, whistling, up and down the streets that had once been his ancestors' meadows, and before that, Indian hunting grounds. You could still find arrowheads everywhere; kids were always hunting for them in the dirt of construction sites, and anyone who broke ground for a garden was sure to unearth at least one or two.

He wore a hat, too — Jay Johnson — a light-colored fedora, and he also walked with his head down, like Felix, the old man who imitated bird calls and sat at Murphy's lunch counter. Jay Johnson, though, walked only at night but in all kinds of weather; in snowstorms, and even in electrical storms, you could hear him, walking, whistling, accompanied by the kettledrums of thunder. Jay Johnson was my age and he was the brainiest kid in our class. He had a photographic memory, and people said he never slept. He kept to himself and won every academic prize in the state, but like all kids who are different, he was the brunt of jokes, and when I think back on him now, I know he must have been miserable. We called him Dracula because he roamed around at night. We called him Jane because of his long white hands, slight frame, and effeminate ways.

DURING THE LAST two years we lived on Cher-Lee Circle — in the late nineteen-sixties — my mother was bedridden. A visiting practical nurse came to the house during the day and gave my mother shots, first Demerol, then morphine, then Dilaudid. After school, at night, I gave the shots myself, at six and ten P.M.

and again at two and six in the morning, and throughout the weekends. My mother was always awake when I went into her room and very anxious, waiting for the shot. A little before two A.M. she would knock on a wall of her bedroom, which shared a wall with mine, with an old walking stick she kept by the bed.

The nurse, a young woman not much older than I, had taught me how to give the injection by practicing on an orange. I would help my mother to the bathroom and back into bed and get her a drink of water and then her shot. Then I would sit beside the bed and read to her with the milkglass light burning until she fell back to sleep. Oftentimes while I sat there, I'd hear Jay Johnson whistling, either on Cher-Lee Circle or Mari-Kay Lane, or sometimes even farther away on the old Little Indian Creek Road. It was so quiet you could almost hear the fog swirling slowly through the yards and around the houses. Just that kind of hush and Jay Johnson whistling.

"Here comes Jay Johnson," my mother would say dreamily, her speech slurred, and then nod off to sleep.

My mother lay in bed for so long, she said she knew the birds by their voices and their expressions. She had names for all of them — there were robins named Frankie and Johnnie and a cardinal named Mortimer Twigg. A little titmouse she called Peter Lawford, and a bobolink was named Robert Frost. My father had hung bird feeders outside my mother's window and a small wire suet cage for the birds who wintered over. There were sparrows, house wrens, and chickadees. Two blue jays, too: Mata Hari and Aphra Behn. My mother knew them all, which ones had migrated back in the spring and which ones hadn't, and she worried about them when they left in the fall for their long journey and fretted about what had become of the ones who never returned.

In the summer, a catbird named Puss nested in the yews and meowed underneath my mother's window. Somewhere far away — the old Johnson barn, I imagined — an owl my mother named Boswell hooted late at night, and every evening we listened for the whippoorwill.

"Will," my mother called him. "Where's Poor Will this evening, do you suppose, Jo?" she'd ask me. In the spring the thrushes came and then the swallows.

One August night not long before my mother died, I heard her call out in a loud voice. I was startled awake, and I hurried next door to her room. She was sitting up in bed, sobbing, with a wild look in her eyes, her bed jacket tangled, her hair disheveled. She reached out her hands to me. They were shaking. "My gloves," she pleaded, "my gloves. Will, give me my gloves! Will, get me my gloves before the dogs get them! They're my best gloves, my kid gloves. Will!" she called out again. "Will!" She pointed and stared at the dresser. In all the commotion, Charles de Gaulle, who slept beside her, where my father used to sleep, began running back and forth on the bed, growling and tearing at the chenille bedspread with his teeth, shaking it wildly back and forth.

My father heard the commotion and came up in his pajamas from downstairs. He'd been sleeping on the couch for months so he could get a good night's rest. "What is it?" he asked. "What is it, Hannah?" he said to my mother. "Johanna," he said to me, "get your mother a drink. Pour your mother a drink of water.

"Hannah," he said to my mother, "Hannah, it's me. It's me, George. George, your husband."

"Will, get me my gloves!" my mother cried out again. "They're over there." She pointed again to the dresser. She was delirious and did not recognize me or my father.

"Who's Will?" I asked my father later as we stood in the hallway after my mother had fallen back to sleep and we had tiptoed out of her room. I was so confused. All I could think of was Poor Will, the whippoorwill.

"Will was her brother," my father whispered, shaking his head. "She must have been dreaming about her brother. The morphine can give you dreams like that, they say. Hallucinations."

And then I remembered him, of course — Will, the handsome cadet in the old tinted photograph in the picture album — my mother's older brother who had died at Pearl Harbor, years before I was born. I don't know when it was exactly because it was so long ago, but somewhere around that time I got the notion of giving myself an injection of morphine, too, back then, years ago on Cher-Lee Circle, when my mother called out for her gloves.

THAT WAS SO long ago, and I had succeeded, for the most part, all these years at trying to forget. Why was it coming back to me now, thousands of miles from home, on a night train in Africa, crossing the Sahara Desert? Suddenly it seemed like so much of my life was so far behind me, temporally and otherwise. Like it had slipped away while I wasn't paying attention. No longer was my life in front of me, full of possibilities, spreading out vast and unknown as the Sahara. I was middle-aged, and I was beginning to feel, to really feel, the limitations and unlikelihoods, the gradual weathering and eroding of dreams, the rounded-off corners and worn-smooth edges of my little life, the ineluctable demise of the body.

Although I felt so much older, it didn't seem like that much time had really passed. Time seemed to have just accumulated, wadded up like hair in a drain. And what about life? Did it really pass? Or was it all there, always there, the whole terrain of it? Were we like stars, visible only at certain times, under certain circumstances, in certain lighting — or the lack of it? Crossing paths, casting shadows, burning, falling, spinning and spiraling, careening through time and space? To make this train, to catch this bus, to make this plane . . . How many lives had I lived in this one incarnation?

It seemed incredible how my life had mutated over the past forty years. I imagined myself as one of those transformer toys that little boys are so adept at manipulating, but instead of a monster truck that changes into a warrior, I was merely human, yet in some ways a fantastic equal in terms of transformation. Look: a teenager in a miniskirt, waiting to see Bob Dylan. Flip, twist, click-click: an old woman on a train. What had happened to Bobbie Flannery from Mari-Kay Lane? And Jay Johnson, the whistler? And all the other boys and girls, men and woman, who had briefly been my partners in this allemande and promenade?

Our junior year in high school, Bobbie's widowed mother died from breast cancer, as my mother would also the following summer. Bobbie went to live with her sister and brother-in-law, and the house Bobbie and her mother had lived in on Mari-Kay Lane was sold. I saw her only a few times after that. The next fall, I went to college in Vermont where I fell helplessly, hopelessly in love with my English lit teacher, a young poet from Berkeley, and gradually, Bobbie and I lost touch.

Twice when Bobbie and I were in high school, we got up at five A.M. and took the bus from Indian Creek into New York City. We took the subway from near the Port Authority down to Washington Square and hung out along Bleecker and Mac-Dougal streets, hoping to see Bob Dylan around the Gaslight Café or the Café Wha? We'd hang out outside the Fillmore East, the Electric Circus, and Gerde's Folk City until we had to leave and catch the last bus home at eleven P.M. And once we even did see Bob Dylan: he was sitting at the counter in the Bleecker Street Café, eating a hamburger. We were on the sidewalk, and we saw him through the window.

The last time I saw Bobbie, though, we didn't go to Greenwich Village. We ate egg salad sandwiches on soggy white bread at Horn & Hardart, then walked around Manhattan, window shopping, half-heartedly admiring the fashions in the windows of Saks, B. Altman, and all the other fancy department stores uptown before saying our goodbyes. A year later, I made a trip to New York City alone, that time for an illegal abortion. No one in my family knew. No one knows. I used the name Rosa Alberghetti.

ON THE MARRAKESH EXPRESS, I pulled up the greasy vinyl shade and flicked off the dim compartment light above my head just as the day was dawning and the white houses in the white sands of Casablanca began flickering by like ghosts. The Atlantic Ocean winked her sharp blue eye, and I blinked back. In the jaw of the harbor, I could make out more and more whitewashed buildings rising up like jagged rows of teeth, jacaranda dangling their wilted corsages like lavender spinach caught between them. Soon, walls draped in bougainvillea and doors chipped blue, protected by the hand of Fatima, flashed by. Phillip stirred and opened his eyes.

"Hey, Jo, where are we? What time is it?" he asked.

"Casablanca," I said. "We made it this far. Nearly five."

"Casablanca," Phillip said. "White house. Casablanca. I love that word."

"Me, too," I said, smoothing his wispy hair. "Casablanca."

"Casablanca."

From a minaret somewhere across the miles of rooftops, a muezzin was chanting, broadcasting the dawn *adhan* across the waking city, calling the sleepers — the faithful sleepers — to morning prayer. To the west, out over the sea, a slender moon was fading, a pale morning star still asleep in her cradle.

Allah is most great . . . the call to prayer begins. It spreads out slowly, hypnotically, like a narcotic, throughout all of Islam . . .

Come to prayer, come to salvation . . .

"Did you get any sleep? Have you been reading all the way?" Phillip asked, sitting up and yawning, rubbing his eyes and stretching his long arms.

"No . . . I . . . I mean . . . yes," I answered, closing my book as the Marrakesh Express squealed and slowed, clanging her bell like the Panama Limited and creeping into the station. "I was reading . . . Raymond Carver."

Here on Earth

HIS SCIENTIFIC NAME was *Rattus norvegicus,* but everyone had their own pet name for him: Ratso, Rat Man, Ratatouille, Mr. President, The King, Baron von Basement.

He was a rat and he lived in the basement, behind the furnace, at 448 Elysian Avenue. The furnace was a big aluminum and sheet metal octopus with eight sprawling tentacles that delivered hot air to the four apartments. Everyone who lived there — Renata Creech in 1-A, old Mrs. Ping across the hall in 1-B, the newlyweds Kurt and Candace upstairs in 2-A, Wendy and Royal in 2-B — had seen the rat when they went down to the cellar to do their laundry, rummage about in their designated storage spaces, or carry in or out their garbage cans.

He was a big rat. Some people mistook him for a cat or a raccoon.

"A groundhog," Candace in 2-A said, describing the pink spaghetti tail.

"No, dear, that would be a possum," Kurt corrected her.

A raccoon was what Renata thought at her first sighting. She saw something big and dark stroll by, hugging the wall like a nun, and then disappearing behind the furnace. He was so slow and nonchalant that Renata wasn't even startled.

"Stomp your feet when you go down the steps," Royal advised Renata, "and he'll stay away. He's as afraid of us as we are of him" — the same thing that Timothy Treadwell had said about grizzlies — "and think how big we are compared to him. We're like, man, we're like, the size of dinosaurs to that little guy. We're like . . . we're like King Kong to him. He's not gonna bother us. Trust me on this. And he has just as much right to be here as we do. *Homo sapiens* have no right trying to eliminate rats.

"We have our big cabbage-size brains," Royal went on, holding his hands out about a foot on either side of his head, "and our nifty opposable thumbs" — wiggling his thumbs in Renata's face — "but they've got native intelligence, which we lack. And they've got resilience, too. And they've got the numbers. In New York City alone, there are twelve rats to every human. That's ninety-six million rats. One female rat can bear two hundred fifty-six babies in one year. It's their des—"

Royal had a way of leaping up on the moral high ground and ranting about every little thing. Renata cut him off with a big smile and a tiny little wave, a hand gesture you might make to say bye-bye to a baby. She backed down the hall, turned, and hurried down the stairs.

Well, if that rat has every right to be here, then why doesn't he cough up his share of the rent? Renata wanted to ask Royal. She was going around to the tenants upstairs trying to drum up some support and a promise to help foot the bill for an exterminator, which she intended to deduct from her rent, although she was certain the landlord would insist the occupants pay for an exterminator themselves. It was early on a Friday evening, and she was hoping for Wendy, not Royal, to answer the door.

Royal. Royal Oaks. What kind of name was that, anyway?

It sounded like the name of a housing development or some swanky resort. *The happy couple will be honeymooning at The Royal Oaks.* Surely that couldn't be his real name. But who would change their name to Royal Oaks? With a sudden cringe, Renata recalled how on her twenty-first birthday she had changed her name, legally, to Blue Indigo.

"Blue Indigo?" Renata's mother had repeated the name and then stood with her mouth hanging open after Renata told her. "And we gave you the most beautiful name. Well, Miss — or is it Mizz? — Blue Indigo, just don't tell your father, or you'll be Miss Black-and-Blue Indigo."

Renata really didn't know anything about the tenants in 2-B. They'd been there for two or three years, but they were hardly ever home. Wendy worked as a biologist with the state's department of environmental protection, and nobody knew what Royal actually did for a living. He was some kind of animal rights activist. There was a rumor that he'd been caught in California — red-handed — breaking into a research laboratory and liberating the rats. And, in fact, that rumor was true, and Renata's suspicions about his name were not unfounded. Royal's real name was Adam, and he had had six rats on his person when the police apprehended him. He pleaded not guilty, then fled. Royal Adam was now working on a campaign in Indian Gap to prevent the construction of an interstate highway that would disturb the habitat of the white-spotted slimy salamander (*Plethodon cylindraceus*). Wendy and Royal headed the group of enraged citizens opposing the proposed corridor.

Royal was always stuffing their mailboxes with flyers about native plants and non-native invasive species. The latest flyer was about purple loosestrife (*Lythrum salicaria*) — a tall, beautiful plant with magenta spikes — and how it had to be eradicated or it would take over the world. Native to Eurasia, purple loosestrife was brought to America by settlers who prized its height and color in their flower gardens, and purple loosestrife seeds were abundant in the tons of dirt that were used as a ballast in ships to keep them stable at sea. A single plant could produce over a million seeds, Royal's brochure stated. It choked out its competitors and had taken over millions of acres of land.

But wait a minute. Weren't white people a non-native invasive species, too? Weren't we the settlers on those ships with the purple loosestrife seeds in our pockets? Didn't we wipe out our competitors all over the world and take over millions of acres of land?

But arguing with Royal was like trying to sell ice to an Eskimo, as Renata's father used to say. Of course, neither Wendy nor Royal were going to help pay for an exterminator. What was Renata thinking when she knocked on their door? They would probably start a nationwide campaign to save the damn rat. She pictured the media camped out on the sidewalk, herself going in and out the building with a coat over her head.

Back in her own apartment after her futile knocking, Renata grabbed the phone book off the top of the refrigerator, flipped to the yellow pages, and plopped down on her couch. Abel Exterminating advertised "no-kill, humane removal of rodents, birds, and small mammals."

She picked up the phone. Maybe she could get Royal and Wendy to help with the bill after all.

"BIG AS A toaster," Abel Blood, the exterminator, said, returning from the basement. "He's a clever one, too, that big rat," he said coming back upstairs where Renata waited in the hall, "but not as clever as us, is he, Vic?" Vic was Abel's assistant, a big guy with a lantern jaw like Jay Leno's, only one hand, and an eye with a mind of its own.

"Don't you worry, ma'am. We'll get that boy," Abel assured Renata.

To Renata, Abel Blood and his sidekick, Vic, did not look clever at all. She would bet on the rat, but she smiled and said,

"Have at it," and they went out to their pickup and returned with a trap the size of a medium-sized dog crate and some cans of Nine Lives.

In spite of a lack of solidarity, Renata had gone ahead and placed the call to Abel Exterminating after Mrs. Ping, startled by the rat, had fallen backwards over her wagon and broken her hip, apparently while Renata was upstairs futilely knocking. Renata was the one who found Mrs. Ping on the basement floor and called 911.

No one even knew that Mrs. Ping could speak English. She always had tissues or big wads of lint stuffed in her ears. She never spoke or made eye contact, and if you spoke or got close to her, she grunted and spit and sometimes farted.

"Rat," Mrs. Ping looked up from the cellar floor and moaned to Renata when she found her. "Big fuckin' rat."

Mrs. Ping had lived in the apartment building even longer than Renata, who had moved in nine years ago, after her divorce from Husband Number Two. Mrs. Ping had looked ancient when Renata moved in, but the funny thing was this: she looked exactly the same after nine years.

For as long as Renata could remember, Mrs. Ping, who was no bigger than a ten-year-old, wore basically the same clothes: a plastic shower cap with daisies; a Black Watch plaid pleated skirt like a Catholic school girl might wear, over a pair of slick pink jogging pants; a long-sleeved Pittsburgh Pirates T-shirt; flesh-colored cotton stockings rolled down around her ankles; and running shoes with glow-in-the-dark stripes and no laces. In rainy weather, Mrs. Ping added a nondescript tan trench coat with belt loops the size of index cards but no belt; in winter, a nubby turquoise coat with three-quarter-length sleeves and some kind of ratty fur collar, and mismatched oven mittens.

How easy it would be to become eccentric, Renata thought. To stop combing your hair and start wearing a shower cap every day like Mrs. Ping, or oven mittens instead of gloves, to just give up the façade of normalcy and its uniforms, to let yourself go, go wild, to swing out farther and farther away from the center. To break wind in public. To stop going to work and just live minimally, live deliberately, like Thoreau said he was going to do when he went to live in the woods. He would "drive life into a corner," he said. He would "suck the marrow" out of it.

Mrs. Ping was known far and wide as the Chinese Bag Lady, although no one knew for certain if she was Chinese. Some people called her Mary Kay because she always carried a large pink plastic shopping bag advertising Mary Kay cosmetics. She was seen all over town, collecting aluminum cans and pop bottles, sorting through garbage cans and dumpsters early in the morning before the garbage trucks arrived. Some days she pulled an old wagon with wooden slats, piled high with cans, magazines, and bottles. Sometimes the wagon was covered with a vinyl shower curtain splattered with cartoonish drawings of black and white cows.

No one knew Mrs. Ping's first name either. Her mailbox said simply F. PING. Some people said she'd been a child prodigy, a famous violinist who had played at Carnegie Hall. Others said she was the widow of a coal magnate, the mistress of a dead president, or the mother of Yoko Ono. Once a year around Thanksgiving, every year without fail, an old black Checker cab in mint condition, with a New York license plate, pulled up in front of 448 Elysian, and a tall man in an overcoat and bowler got out of the back with a briefcase and visited Mrs. Ping for about fifteen minutes while the chauffeur sat with the car running, smoking and reading a tabloid newspaper. That was the only company, as far as anyone knew, that Mrs. Ping ever received.

After the ambulance took Mrs. Ping away, the building seemed strangely quiet. Although there was never a sound coming out of Mrs. Ping's apartment, the silence from 1-B now seemed enormous. It was a weekend, and no one was home in the apartments upstairs, which was not unusual, and Renata realized that in all the years she'd lived there, she'd never once been totally alone in the evening. Although Mrs. Ping combed the city from daybreak nearly every morning sometimes until dusk, she was always home at night. You couldn't see in any of her windows because they were covered with something like wax or soap, but there was always a warm yellow glow behind them, and the same beam of bright light shone like gold bullion from underneath her door.

That night, after Mrs. Ping's fall, Renata hadn't been able to sleep. Her feet were cold and she wanted to go down to the basement to get her favorite fuzzy socks out of the dryer, but she was afraid of the rat. She stood in her pajamas and robe at the top of the cellar steps, smoking a cigarette, considering a quick dash down the stairs and back, when she noticed that Mrs. Ping's door was slightly ajar. She put her hand on the knob to close it and then hesitated.

She'd never been in Mrs. Ping's apartment. Should she take a little peek? What if someone — a relative or a burglar, maybe the mysterious man in the topcoat and bowler, or Yoko Ono herself — was inside?

Nah. It was totally dark and quiet. Renata returned to her apartment, put her headlamp on, and slipped back into the hall. She stood a moment listening, then stepped into Mrs. Ping's apartment and closed the door.

She was not prepared for what greeted her: a wall.

A floor-to-ceiling wall made out of crushed tin cans for pillars and bricks that looked to be about 8 x 4 x 2 inches, stacks of folded newspapers and cardboard from butter boxes and cigarette cartons, wrapped tightly with twine. There were small windows in the wall, which seemed to be woven out of butter wrappers and pieces of wax paper, and colored bottles stuck in here and there among the bricks so that their bases glimmered like bright medallions in the beam of Renata's headlamp.

Worked into the wall were all kinds of trinkets and ornaments: clock faces and motherboards, piano keys, batteries, sunglasses, dominoes and ticket stubs, doll limbs, stamps, and coins. There was a thick mat on the floor with an elaborate design, which, upon examination, Renata determined to be braided of rags and strips of plastic soda bottles. She followed the wall as it turned and snaked through the apartment like the Serpent Mound in southern Ohio.

In the living room and dining room the wall formed aisles like in a library, only narrower. There wasn't a stick of furniture or anything utilitarian in sight. In the bedroom the wall formed a spiral like a chambered nautilus (*Nautilus pompilius*), which opened up into something like a tiny chapel with a ceiling, where aluminum foil and little pieces of wrapping paper had been carefully pieced together to form moons, stars, and constellations. Renata recognized Lyra, Orion, and Pegasus.

Hundreds of tiny mobiles made of pieces of broken jewelry and hair barrettes spun and twinkled from twine, twist ties, and fishing line at different heights from the ceilings.

Sometimes as she followed the wall it stopped dead, and Renata had to back up and take another route. What it was, Renata realized with awe and panic, was a maze. A maze made of recycled cans and glass bottles, newspapers, magazines, plastic, all things humans discarded. It was wonderful and fantastic beyond belief. It was a recycling installation, all things found, forgotten, and forsaken.

It wasn't the rat's fault Mrs. Ping had fallen. Renata didn't blame him, really. It was the landlord's fault for not keeping the basement rat-free, for not getting a dumpster for the building, for making them keep their garbage cans in the basement, for not filling in the holes in the foundation and not boarding up the defunct garage doors with their eight-inch gap under them, and for not having an exterminator come on a regular basis.

There were waterbugs, too, big as Matchbox cars. They were activated by light and zoomed around like bumper cars whenever you came home at night and flicked on the overheads. Waterbugs! Nothing but a euphemism for roaches. Mr. Euphemism, Renata called the landlord, a middle-aged man with a mullet, a man she had once found attractive and — she cringed at the thought — had even slept with on two occasions — a married man named Marvin Hoppenthal.

Everybody who lived at 448 Elysian had to deal with the roaches. The roaches could fly, too, Renata had recently discovered, although they couldn't fly well. They flew with the proficiency of, say, a chicken. Renata had put up with them for years. Roach motels were on her shopping list as frequently as detergent. She thought she had the roaches under control. She thought she knew them well, and then one day she bent down to pick up with a pair of hemostats what she thought was a dead roach and damn if the thing didn't hop and fly behind the couch. All these years, and she never knew they had wings.

All the tenants had roach motels under their couches and behind their toilets, sinks, stoves, and refrigerators. In closets and corners. Take away the furniture and appliances and the place would look like a roach vacation land: roach motel after motel after motel. Renata had one of her ideas that these roach motels could come in different styles, like those little lighted houses that you saw everywhere at Christmas — Dickens's Village or something like that they were called. There could be a church and a courthouse, a theater and a library, some kind of tavern, a café, and a bookstore. Maybe a haberdashery. They'd be ceramic and pretty, not ugly, disposable cardboard boxes, brown so as to recede into the corners. And you wouldn't have to hide them; you could collect and display them. They'd come with little pills of roach poison that you dropped down, say, the chimney of the tavern or the steeple of the church.

Or they could be modeled after real motels and hotels: Best Western, Hilton, Comfort Inn, Super 8, and the chains could sell replicas in their lobbies or give them as favors at conventions instead of mousepads, coffee mugs, and paperweights with silk-screened logos — things everybody threw away.

This wonderful idea had come to her in a dream. Renata sat up and wrote it down in the notebook on her bedside table, where she kept track of all her inventions. It was number 189, right below the water-walking Jesus bath toy.

#188. Water-Walking Jesus bath toy

- dashboard Jesus
- chamber
- cork
- baking soda
- some kind of weight. Ball bearing?

Renata's dream was to be an inventor. As a baby, she was fascinated by her grandfather's metal address book. It was a slim brushed-aluminum rectangle about four inches wide and eight inches long, with the alphabet and a red sliding pointer down one side. The slightest pressure on a thumb pedal at the bottom made the contraption flip open to an index card of the addressees with last names that began with the letter indicated by the pointer.

Renata broke it deliberately when she was three, disassembled it when she was four.

She'd been writing down her inventions for years. She had to write them down so she'd remember them since they always came to her in dreams. She couldn't wait to get to work to tell her friend Jack about the Dickens's Village roach motels.

He loved making up ads for crazy things. He'd make Renata a pretend ad for the roach motels. Probably pull down off the

Web one of those Thomas Kinkade paintings of a house that looks like there's a terrific fire raging inside, layer on a Bates Bed-and-Breakfast sign out front, a family of roaches with luggage approaching the door, Anthony Perkins peeping out from behind a lace curtain in one of the upstairs windows, and the slogan THEY CHECK IN BUT THEY DON'T CHECK OUT.

As RENATA HAD predicted, Abel Exterminating did not succeed in capturing the rat. Every morning for three days, Abel and Vic returned to 448 Elysian to find the cage empty and the Nine Lives gone, tin and all.

"Peculiar," Abel said. "Never seen anything like it. Of course we're going to have to charge you anyway for our time, Ms. Creech," he said in one breath.

"Yup, time is money," added Vic, scratching his back on the doorjamb.

Over the next two days Renata encountered the rat twice. Very early on Tuesday morning, the rat stood by the furnace the way someone might loiter outside a cigar shop, as Renata descended the stairs to put in her wash before she left for work. She turned and hurried back upstairs, dirty laundry and all.

That evening, on her way out to the grocery store, she walked around to the back of the building and peeped through the tiny window in the cellar door. There lay the rat stretched out like a cat not three feet from the threshold. He had made himself at home, that rat. He had adapted. He knew the people who lived at 448 Elysian, their screams, their footsteps, and contrary to what Royal had assured Renata, the rat was not even one tiny bit afraid of any of them. Still, somehow he had managed to elude the Mensa duo of Abel and Vic.

It was during that trip to the grocery store that Renata spotted the Pied Piper's van. As she was parking, the Pied Piper was just pulling out of the space next to the one she was pulling into.

The van was dented and white, with an airbrushed painting on the side of an elf playing a flute and a parade of grinning rats skipping along behind him. In the foreground was a rushing stream with leaping rainbow trout (*Oncorhynchus mykiss*), and in the background a quaint village with townspeople dancing around a maypole.

Although on Wednesday Renata was expecting a small man in green leggings and a pointed hat, a man with a little goatee and a silver flute, the Pied Piper turned out to be a big, clean-shaven man in a gray jumpsuit with a huge stuffed rat under his arm. The Pied Piper's name was Lance Flemming. The rat he called "the decoy."

The Pied Piper showed up at ten P.M., as he'd told Renata over the phone he would. He would stay, he said, until he had the rat, which he estimated to be before midnight. Renata would pay him one hundred dollars, and he'd take the rat away, down to the river to a place he knew out near Wally Walker's car lot on the Old Indian River Road. He'd let the rat go, and that would be that.

He hoped the music wouldn't keep her or any of the other residents awake, the Pied Piper said, and he hoped she understood that he had to play the music at a certain volume or the whole thing was a waste of time.

Renata showed him to the basement and wondered if he was married.

The decoy was really a huge animated mouse from a Macy's window display in Newark, New Jersey, which the Pied Piper had "borrowed" when he worked in the store's stockroom one Christmas season many years ago. Lance had inserted a CD player with tiny, powerful speakers inside the mouse. As the music played, the mouse danced, moving his arms this way and that, bobbing his head, and kicking his legs. Lance had a patent pending on his invention, along with testimonials from over twenty-five customers. Would Renata agree to compose a short testimonial once the rat was captured?

"Yes, yes, of course," she said. She fantasized about sharing some of her own inventions with the Pied Piper, perhaps collaborating with him, maybe patenting them together. He wore no wedding ring.

He had many kinds of music on his mixed CDs, he told Renata, which he'd made himself: classical, rock, alternative, techno, rap. He had to assess the situation before he could choose the correct CD. Sometimes rats came right up to the decoy during the first song. The longest holdout was just short of two hours.

Back in her apartment, Renata wondered what kind of music *her* rat preferred. She fancied that he was rather highbrow since she listened quite often to public radio. Mozart's *Magic Flute*? Maybe Jean-Pierre Rampal? Or maybe something jazzy — Herbie Mann?

To her astonishment and dismay, disco began to blare from the basement: Sister Sledge, "We Are Family." Michael Jackson, "Billie Jean." K. C. and the Sunshine Band, "Celebration." The Pointer Sisters, "I'm So Excited." The artist formally known as Prince with "1999," and Captain and Tennille's "Muskrat Love." It was like a bad flashback of a Casey Kasem countdown from a quarter-century ago.

Renata hated disco. She turned up public radio to try to drown it out, but it was one of those dreadful pledge drives, more annoying than any advertising. Finally, she stuffed her ears with cotton balls and took a shower. It was eleven-thirty. Wouldn't you know it, not only was her rat a disco rat, he was of the two-hour variety.

When she was getting dressed, the music stopped.

A few minutes later, the Pied Piper knocked on her door.

"He came out to 'Stayin' Alive,'" he said. "You know, the

theme song from *Saturday Night Fever*." The Pied Piper was unabashedly pleased with his success and grinned ear to ear as he
gave Renata the news.

His smile was charming.

Renata pictured the rat in a white satin suit, one front leg
raised high, strutting his stuff in front of the furnace like John
Travolta; the Pied Piper, similarly dressed, standing at the bottom of the stairs; and a twenty-years-younger, thirty-pounds-
lighter version of herself in teased hair, strappy high-heeled
shoes, and a slinky, sparkly, spandex dress appearing on the
landing.

"Here he is, ma'am," the Pied Piper said, holding up the cage.

The rat looked at Renata and screamed.

His mouth was so pink it looked like he'd been sucking on a
fireball. His teeth were the color of a school bus. Red and yellow.
Red and yellow. From that moment, every time she drove past a
Sheetz convenience center or a McDonald's, Renata would see
that rat's terrified face and hear his blood-curdling scream.

Not only had he screamed, he'd made eye contact momentarily before he screamed. He looked *right* into Renata's eyes
with a terrified, accusing, almost human stare. In fact, for a split
second, he reminded her of somebody: Tom Cruise.

The rat screamed bloody murder, and Renata screamed
bloody murder back. She didn't even know she was screaming.
She didn't even know she *could* scream. She'd never heard herself scream before. Probably the last time she'd screamed was at
her birth. It was some kind of primal response, something deep
inside her that she'd never even come close to getting in touch
with, even during anger-management training.

Once, years ago, she'd almost drowned, and even then it
never occurred to her to scream. She raised her arm and waved.
Husband Number Two was there by the pool. He waved back
from his lounge chair and smiled, sipping a drink with a little

green umbrella. Not until her head went under did he dive in and save her, taking the time to remove his toupee and place it neatly under his towel.

She'd forgotten all about that. She did owe him something after all.

The moment the rat screamed, Renata started running around in circles in her apartment, screaming and screaming, lifting her knees up high like a majorette, flailing her arms. Just because a rat had looked her in the eye and screamed. Thinking back, she saw herself at that moment doing the same frantic dance as an Indian chief she'd once seen at a powwow, a guy dressed in chicken feathers and thigh-high buckskin boots, chanting, and shaking a rattle.

The Pied Piper set down the cage in the hallway, came to Renata, and took her in his arms.

"There, there now," he soothed her. "It's all right, ma'am. That's all right. Happens all the time," he kept saying. He drew her to his chest and smoothed her hair. Renata imagined that he kissed the crown of her head, but he didn't.

She was thoroughly embarrassed. After the Pied Piper left, standing alone in the kitchen with a shot of bourbon and a cigarette, she remembered a woman she had seen on a television talk show when she was a teenager. The show was about post-traumatic stress disorder, and the woman was the only survivor of a horrific automobile accident that had killed her three traveling companions, one of whom was her fiancé. The survivor said that she stepped out of the car and saw her friends' bodies on the road, tossed about haphazardly like big rag dolls. Everything was perfectly quiet except for a hissing sound like a large teakettle. She leaned against a snowbank and was aware of a wild animal howling close by. Above the snowbank towered a billboard with a larger-than-life Cybill Shepherd in a black velvet gown, leaning forward seductively and offering an aquarium-size glass filled with ice cubes and amber liquid. Only when the EMT team arrived and a medic touched the survivor's arm did the howling stop, and it was some time later before she realized that there never was a wild animal at the scene of the accident.

The woman on the talk show ended up marrying the medic, and they had twin daughters who came on stage in matching tam-o'-shanters, along with their father, and kissed their mother.

That night, after the rat had been trapped, Renata dreamed about the Pied Piper. They were in Giant Eagle, shopping together — with one cart — and within the bizarre architecture of dreams, the fresh fish department was also the U.S. Patent Office. A wooden sign hanging from brass hardware above the counter displayed a fish on a bicycle in bas-relief and invited customers to pick a number, protect their inventions, and eat more fish. In the dream, Renata was young again, with a boyish haircut and wearing the same dress made out of an India print bedspread she had worn when she married Husband Number One, a ceremony that had taken place within the trunk of a two-thousand-year-old redwood (*Sequoia sempervirens*). So much for symbolism.

The next evening Renata called the Pied Piper. She had spent the whole day preparing a little speech. She was calling, she would say, just to make sure he had made it out to the river and that the rat was free. Then she'd casually ask if he liked Mexican food and suggest they meet at Los Mariachis for a margarita.

She drank a glass of grapefruit juice to purify her vocal cords and held the phone to her heart a brief moment before taking a deep breath and actually dialing. A child answered. Momentarily startled by this unanticipated development, Renata hesitated a second but regained her composure in a flash, cleared her throat, and asked in her most grownup, most businesslike voice, "May I speak to the Pied Piper, Mr. Lance Flemming, please?"

"Da-deeeeeeeeeeee!" the child screamed, and Renata hung up, screaming herself in shock, disappointment, and abject humiliation.

THE RIF (reduction in force, a corporate euphemism for layoff) took place on a Friday afternoon, and the dismissals were immediate. Savvy human resources departments operated this way out of fear that those dismissed might sabotage their computers or remaining employees might plot an insurrection on company time.

It had been a long, stressful week: first Mrs. Ping, then the screaming rat, and the previous night the screaming child. An hour before quitting time the mail-notification bell dinged on Renata's computer. The email was from the company president, Harold Burke, who was in the main office in Pittsburgh. No one had ever seen Harold Burke. They knew him only by his power-tie photograph in the lobby and his name on corporate documents. He could have been a mannequin like people had said of Nancy Reagan.

The elusive Harold Burke sent out an email once a year, at the end of the year, a nauseating canned message wishing everyone happy new year and telling them what valuable employees they were and how Optimum was happy to have them as members of its corporate family. This afternoon the subject on Harold Burke's email was one hyphenated word: THANK-YOU.

Dear Ms. Creech,

Thank you for your many years of service at Optimum Communications. I am sorry to inform you that, due to a loss of revenue in 2006, your position has been eliminated. A member of building security will stop by your cubicle at 4:30 P.M. to escort you from the building. Please take all your personal belongings with you at that time. Anything left behind will be destroyed, and you will not be allowed access to the building after 4:30 P.M. today.

As you leave the building, you will be given a packet that contains important information about your legal rights concerning this separation, the filing of unemployment, and the continuation of health benefits through COBRA. A check in the amount of your severance pay is in the mail.

Once again, I thank you for your hard work and years of service, and I apologize personally for any inconvenience this separation might cause you.

Good luck and have a nice weekend. Go Steelers!

Sincerely,
Harold Burke, President and CEO,
Optimum Communications
A Worldwide Leader in Effective Business Communications

Renata took a choppy breath and read the email again. It had to be a joke. She'd worked there for fourteen years. Surely it was a joke. It was from Jack. It was a prank email from Jack. It had to be. She checked the sender's adress. It was Harold Burke's for sure. She checked the distribution list. "Dear Valued Employees" it said. Somehow Jack had sabotaged Harold Burke's email account and sent out the email to all the employees. Renata printed out the message and looked at it again. She laughed a nervous little laugh. It was awfully quiet in her neck of the cube farm. She stepped out into the aisle. Many other people, including Jack, were standing there silently, holding a piece of paper.

Hours later, they were at Los Mariachis, empty pitchers of margaritas stuck to the table, guacamole and tortilla chips stuck between their teeth. Renata, Jack, Teresa, Bill, Bobbie, Penny, and Carla: "Valued Employees," all. They were drunk, all of them, sitting in a curved booth in the front window. Across the street a digital sign advertised Tom Jones's "The Tiger's Back" tour that night, a few blocks away at the civic center. Tom Jones was shown in a white shiny shirt open to his sternum, displaying a thick pelt of hair like a beaver's and a gold necklace the size of a tire chain.

"Hey, let's go," Jack said. "Come on, everybody. It will be a riot. Let's go! Let's go! Let's not cry in our beer. Let's celebrate! The first day of the rest of our lives! We're free, free at last!"

"Yeah, the first day of the rest of our lives without jobs," Penny added. "Free to kill ourselves."

Teresa, Bill, Carla, and Penny copped out and called a cab. Jack, Renata, and Bobbie made their way to the concert.

At the civic center, women — hundreds, maybe a thousand — were pouring in the doors.

"Oh, gawd, I *love* it," Jack said, buying the three of them tickets.

The lights dimmed and Tom Jones appeared on stage, looking in the distance like a little action figure in a white jumpsuit. As soon as he started singing — "It's Not Unusual" — it started. Women everywhere began screaming and throwing underwear at the stage. Renata had heard of women taking off their thongs and throwing them to Sting and Mick Jagger, but this was a horse of a different size. These women were *old*. They were in their fifties, sixties, and seventies even, and their undergarments were *not* thongs.

It was like an explosion in a lingerie factory. Captured in the colored lights, big underpants floated down from the balconies like behemoth butterflies. It looked like D-day. Some were flowered, some were lace, some were glow-in-the-dark. Some were autographed and had phone numbers written on them in thick magic marker or glitter. Some had notes, photographs, or love letters pinned to them. Almost all of them were enormous. Most of them had inflated balloons — or inflated condoms — or little homemade parachutes made out of handkerchiefs or napkins attached to them. Some were leather and fell like cannon-balls. Caught in the underpants storm, Renata tried to recall the result of Galileo's famous experiment and wondered what kind of skivvies he had on up there in the Tower of Pisa.

A pair of pink nylon briefs the size of a pup tent floated down from the upper balcony and landed on Renata's head. They were doused in a stinky cologne Renata recognized as Ambush. She nearly passed out before she could get out from under them.

Jack was screaming incoherently, and to her alarm, Bobbie was wiggling out of her pantyhose and tying them in a knot.

Renata was sobering up, and she was appalled.

"Here on Earth," Renata's father used to say to her when she was a teenager and trying to sneak out of the house in a mini-skirt and kohl. "Here on Earth," he'd say to her, "we don't dress like that. Here on Earth we wear clothes. Get back upstairs, missy, and put some clothes on, and while you're up there, wash your face."

Or, "Here on Earth," he'd say to Renata's brother if he mouthed off. "Here on Earth, buddy, we don't talk like that. Here on Earth we talk with civility."

"Here on Earth," she could hear her father saying now. "Here on Earth we don't take off our underpants in public and throw them at some Welsh has-been on a stage."

Renata's father had worked a furnace in a glass factory all his life. Every payday for twenty years, he took his paycheck and a gunnysack to the bank and got his entire pay in quarters. Every Friday night he rolled the quarters into red wrappers and nailed them shut in wooden boxes that nails came in. The boxes were locked in Renata's parents' bedroom. In 1976, when Renata was fifteen, her father bought them a new house in the suburbs, a modest house, a pink ranch-style house like on the back cover of The Band's album *Big Pink*.

Her father drove to the bank in his old pickup, taking Renata's brother along to help carry the wooden boxes. Somehow the newspaper got wind of this, and the next morning, Renata's father and brother were on the front page of the *Times Leader,* lugging the boxes into the bank. The headline read, "Local Man Buys House with Rolls of Quarters."

Renata was horrified. She almost died from embarrassment. She refused to go to school for days. Even after her father was dead and she was grown and married, they were still known as The Quarter Family, their house The Quarterhouse.

Once when she was a teenager and still lived in Big Pink, she'd gone to a bra-burning. In fact, she *wore* a bra to the burning with the intention of keeping it on, and a thick, baggy sweatshirt so no one could tell. She liked her bras, actually. She liked the support and warmth, so she stopped at a Goodwill the day before and bought a bra about her size from the dollar bin. What difference did it make? She wanted to protest something but she wasn't sure what. It wasn't bras. It was just something about life, about the way women were treated. About everything wrong with the world.

At the bra-burning, women of all ages and bra sizes stripped off their shirts and threw them as well as their bras on the bonfire. They strutted around baring their breasts, holding up their arms in victory like Channel 9 wrestlers and hollering like coxswains.

"Here on Earth," she said to herself then.

The media was there, too, of course, and dozens of women were arrested for public nudity. Renata stayed back in the crowd, never trying to make it to the fire to toss in her Goodwill purchase.

"Here on Earth," she said to herself again as Tom Jones broke into "What's New Pussycat?" and one thousand post-menopausal women went bonkers.

Finally, at Jack's urging, Renata gave up and followed suit. She reached under her skirt, hooked her thumbs into her underwear, and tugged.

"Here on Earth," she said with a fling.

"What?" Jack screamed into her ear. "What?"

UNDERPANTS COVERED THE floor like leaves after an October tornado. Renata, Jack, and Bobbie shuffled through them toward the exit. *Life is long and weird,* Renata thought. Two nights ago, a rat the size of a bowling bag had looked right in her eyes and screamed, and at this time last night, she was fast asleep, her clothes for work laid out neatly on the chair beside her bed. Little did she know . . .

One day you could be working at the same job you've had for years, and the next day filling out an application for a senior greeter position at Wal-Mart. One minute you could be making art, and the next, lying at the bottom of the stairs with a broken hip like Mrs. Ping, who had had a hip replacement and was still in unstable condition.

In the parking lot of Los Mariachis, Bobbie, Jack, and Renata hugged each other, commiserated, and went their separate ways. Renata felt cold and weird without her underwear. She wrapped her coat around her and shivered as she unlocked her car door. She was wide awake and decided to take a detour instead of driving straight home. Lately, she'd had this urge for some reason to see Big Pink again. Why not now? She crossed the Pleasant Street Bridge and drove out the Old Indian River Road and turned into Johnson's Orchard, the development where the house was that her father had bought with quarters. She hadn't been back in years.

She turned on to Cher-Lee Circle. There it was on the right. The little hemlock trees she'd helped her father plant along the street nearly thirty years ago now formed a fifteen-foot-high hedge, obscuring the house almost completely. Renata pulled in the driveway and turned off the headlights, leaving the engine running. The house was dark inside, but a gaslight glowed by the walk and another by the front entrance. A welcome flag hung limply from a pole by the front door, and a redwood deck had been built out over part of the driveway, off the bedrooms that used to be Renata's and her brother's.

The property was fancily landscaped with squat shrubs and flagstones, and a privacy fence in the back — an extension of the deck — suggested a pool.

And the house wasn't pink anymore, she noted sadly. It was white, maybe ivory.

Her father had paid thirty thousand dollars for the house thirty-three years ago: a fortune, a truck bed full of quarters. How many quarters, how many trucks, would it take to buy this place today?

A light came on in the garage. Renata quickly turned her headlights back on, put the car in reverse, and backed out of the driveway. Along the Old Indian River Road, past Wally Walker's, she pulled off in the Kiwanis Club picnic area and walked the few feet down the pea gravel path to the river's edge.

She wondered if this was where the Pied Piper had taken the rat, if he really had released him. Maybe he had left him in the cage and just drowned him. And why not? He was vermin, after all, wasn't he? And who would know, and what difference would it make? Two hundred fifty-six offspring per female rat per year.

She wanted to see the rat again. She wanted to be startled. She had the same gnawing feeling as when she was a kid and had this urge to shuffle around on the living room carpet in her slick-soled Mary Janes and then touch the television set. Her parents kept telling her to cut it out, but she couldn't. She loved the spark and zap. She needed them. She did it when they weren't looking. She got up in the middle of the night and tiptoed down the stairs in her p.j.'s, Mary Janes in hand. And then one day the Mary Janes were gone, and in their place were rubber-soled penny loafers.

Renata gave a little whistle. "Ratso, Ratso," she called quietly.

What she wanted was to look in his face again and tell him she was sorry. Sorry she had fucked up his life. What right did she have to evict him?

She wanted him to make eye contact again and scream.

What she really wanted was to scream again herself.

Back at 448 Elysian, the apartments were dark and all the re-served-for-residents parking places empty. Kurt and Candace were probably out partying, and Royal and Wendy out making the world a better place for white-spotted slimy salamanders or ridding the planet of purple loosestrife.

And Mrs. Ping? Mrs. Ping had slipped into a coma. In a few days she'd be dead.

Renata parked her car and climbed the stairs. The hall light had burned out again. Damn. She fumbled a moment to fit her key in the lock, then gave up and turned around, opened the door to 1-B, and felt her way along the wall.

Lately

LATELY, I HAVE BEEN thinking a great deal about something a friend of mine from years ago told me. This friend, whose name was Melissa, said that within each of us is a landscape, a kind of spiritual topography that resonates with our physical being like a natural harmony in perfect thirds. If we don't find our spiritual landscape in life, Melissa said, our souls knock about in discord with our surroundings, and we often find ourselves inexplicably agitated, buzzing through life like a bee in a jar.

Mountain, prairie, ocean, desert, city, *other:* those were the basic spiritual landscapes Melissa described. This *other* spiritual landscape was any variation or combination of the five basic types. There was a river scheme and a terrain dominated primarily by ice, and other internal landscapes were based on weather patterns or botanies like deciduous, evergreen, and succulent. It was all very complex, like astrology, which made my head spin.

According to Melissa, you could have, say, a water spirit or a spirit that thrived on the yearly turning and falling of leaves.

Your soul might crave these things, might need them just to squeak by. And it was complicated further by degrees and angles of sunshine and amounts of precipitation. The length of days, according to the earth's meridians, somehow corresponded to the wavelengths of auras, and there was something to do, too, with the phases of the moon and the dancing of the spheres. And if you were not at rest in any place, then chances were that you were some old, nomadic soul. A sojourner. Maybe a homeless person whose address changes with serendipity, chance, and weather.

This was the early eighties, and people were caught up in all kinds of things: Chinese and esoteric astrology, tarot, the Enneagram and the *I Ching,* runes, numerology, chakras, color and light therapy, crystals, spirit guides, past lives, totems, angels, and even aliens among us. On one occasion, I'd gone on a day trip with a carful of women to see a psychic in West Virginia named Miss Donna. Miss Donna told me things that turned out to be true. She said I would be married more than once and that my daughter, Frieda, who was a toddler then, would have a difficult adolescence and young adulthood but that I should not worry because Frieda would survive. That was the word Miss Donna used, *survive.*

I was distressed, and I was beginning to suspect that Lee was being unfaithful again. On the ride back to Indian Gap I felt so panicky I could hardly breathe. I sat behind the driver, Karin Pugh, with the window down and my face in the hot, dirty breeze. Melissa was beside me, doused in patchouli, and next to her was Renata Creech. Renata, who wore her hair in a brush cut like a boy's, had changed her name to Blue Indigo, in honor, she said, of the beautiful blue birthmark on the back of her neck, a mark called a stork bite, which she had spent her youth despising. A few years earlier, a gypsy at a carnival in North Carolina had told Renata that her birthmark was a sign and that she was destined to meet up with her spiritual tribe: others marked the same way. What she had to do was display the sign so they could find her.

On the ride back, right before we got on the interstate, we stopped at a convenience store and bought a twelve-pack of beer and two four-packs of wine coolers, some candy bars, Slim Jims, and Fritos, and after two wine coolers, I began to relax a little and listen to what Miss Donna had told the others, but when my turn came — I was last — I leaned forward and told a complete lie. A big whopper. I said that the psychic had told me that Lee and I would have another baby, a boy, and that Frieda would grow up to be a famous painter or singer, and that in a few years, we'd buy a house with a lot of glass and a swimming pool, far from Indian Gap, out west somewhere like Colorado.

Back then, you couldn't go to anyone's house for dinner without someone mentioning Shirley MacLaine or Jane Roberts. Before that it had been Carlos Castaneda and Gurdjieff and Baba this or Baba that. In fact, Lee and I had a dog we'd named Gurdjieff as a joke. According to the Enneagram, I was a four, with something called a five wing. That was some kind of creative, though private and analytical-type, personality, and I was secretly quite proud of the creative core, thinking I was destined to do something great in the arts — perhaps paint. (Drawing the human figure seemed to come naturally to me, and once I'd won a statewide art contest for a pastel of my mother playing the piano.) Or maybe I'd be a singer like Joni Mitchell; people used to say I had a singing voice like hers. I always sang the solos in choir and in our high school chorus, and there were accomplished musicians in my family; it was in my genes, I thought. But I never could decide which to pursue — drawing or music — and so I became neither an artist nor a musician. Twice I'd bought a used acoustic guitar, but I never learned more than a few chords, and the only song I was ever able to memorize the chord progressions to was "The Night They Drove Old Dixie Down."

On the Enneagram, Lee was a three, a competitive, success-oriented person who paid great attention to details and appearances. The definition suited him. Lee had made a lot of money illicitly when he was young, but he was no dummy. He invested in real estate, buying up farmland cheap and backing developers, turning himself into a successful businessman while he continued to live the high life. And he was an observer, too, especially of women. I thought we were compatible because according to *Sun Signs/Moon Signs,* we had the same moon: moon in Virgo, the lovers' moon.

I WAS TRYING to figure out what was the matter with me back then when Melissa told me about spiritual landscapes. I had begun having panic attacks in public, and it was getting harder and harder for me to go outside. Melissa was trying to help; she was a kind of natural healer, interested in everything from herbs and reflexology to aura cleansing, magnetic therapy, and exorcism. She was one of those soft, matronly types. "Granola girls," Lee called them. Not his type. She wore her hair in braids and dressed in wraparound India print skirts or harem pants made from yards and yards of fabric with bells and beads and embroidery on the cuffs, peasant blouses with poet sleeves and lace-up bodices, thick purple socks and Birkenstocks.

Even getting the mail across the road was difficult for me then, like swimming the English Channel it seemed, so I always sent Frieda for it, watching the road from the kitchen window and blowing a whistle when it was safe for her to run across. At first, she could barely reach up to the box. When I had to get the mail myself — if I was waiting for a check, say, and Frieda was in school — I'd stand in the kitchen, sometimes for hours, trying to get up the courage to go out. I'd smoke cigarette after cigarette and now and then go into the bathroom and take a little swig of Jack Daniel's from a bottle I kept hidden in the toilet tank. From the kitchen I could see the big silver mailbox on its sturdy pressure-treated post across the road. It reminded me of a gladiator, its red flag a bloody battle-axe.

IT OCCURRED TO me as Melissa talked on and on about these spiritual landscapes — she'd brought a book with photographs and colorful illustrations — that this wasn't the first time in my life I was having panic attacks about going outside. I remembered that as a child I was often frightened, especially in big places like parks and department stores. I'd feel dizzy and nauseous, more so if my mother wasn't nearby. I always felt this way in my grandmother's house, too, which was big and hollow, and where I was put to bed in a room by myself at the end of the hall, with the dark shades drawn and the door clicked shut. In that room, I couldn't swallow, couldn't breathe.

One time my family took a day trip to Ocean City, and when we got there, my brothers raced from the car toward the breakers, screaming with delight and dragging their inflatable rafts to the water, but I crouched down on the floor of the backseat and begged to stay in the car. My father pulled me out by my arm. It was, after all, probably ninety degrees outside. I felt that same panic in movie theaters, or in any space that was unfamiliar. If my mother was with me, she'd sit me on her knee and put one hand on my back and her other hand on my chest, holding me together until my heart slowed down. She'd smooth my hair and press me against her and say, "There now, there, there, my little teapot."

As Melissa read the different landscapes to me, I was supposed to close my eyes and picture each one, and then pick the one that "spoke to me." We were drinking Bartles & Jaymes, a sickeningly sweet carbonated wine drink. "Real men don't drink wine coolers," we used to say and laugh as we twisted off the tops. It was somehow more respectable for a woman to buy a four-pack of wine coolers than a six-pack of beer. It was more "ladylike," and you didn't have to go to a state liquor store to get them; you could get them in any grocery store. I remember this because I drank a lot of wine coolers back then. They can make you really sick.

WHEN MELISSA READ the mountain definition, I remembered my room as a child. I saw mountains — the Indian Mountains — out my window. They rippled toward the horizon, growing bluer with each diminution in that amazing way that everything on the horizon looks blue, the illusion of the shortening of color waves in the spectrum, Lee told me, created by the curvature of the earth. My brothers saw the Indian Mountain range, too, out their bedroom window, but then when my youngest brother, Carey, was a Boy Scout, he went to the Dakotas. The Badlands. He came home and said, "I love it out there. I'm going to move there when I grow up and live there forever." He talked about the Badlands with an enthusiasm we had never known him to exhibit about anything. No one in our family could understand his great attraction to the American West, unless it was the romanticism of cowboy movies and television westerns. We had no roots there in the Dakotas, no abiding claim. Now I think that Carey had stumbled upon his interior landscape. He recognized it immediately, like you recognize an old friend or relative you haven't seen in a month of Sundays, and he has lived there out in the Badlands, happily I suppose, ever since. I don't know for sure; I haven't seen him lately.

My second husband, Isaac, loved the desert. He said to me not long after we met, "You have never seen the stars, Gloria, you have never glimpsed the wonders of the firmament, until you've spent a night in the desert.

"Come with me," Isaac said. "Come with me to Chaco Canyon."

But I never went, and eventually he went alone and stayed. Still, I love the word *firmament*, and whenever I hear it, I think sadly of Isaac and how things would have been different if I'd stayed in treatment that time. I never went with Isaac because I was afraid of the desert and its gazillion stars. In the back of my mind still hangs a postcard that a guy named Bill had push-pinned to his cubicle wall when we both worked at the ad agency. On the postcard was a photograph of outerspace taken from a satellite. The card was mostly black with a spray of stars like a salt spill on a black tablecloth, a few planets the size of hominy. YOU ARE HERE the postcard said in white bold-face Helvetica, an arrow pointing to the spray of white dots. I couldn't look at that card, and I always closed my eyes when I passed by that wall of Bill's cubicle, or I took another route to the john so as to avoid that photograph entirely.

I heard that Eagles song in my head when Isaac made his desert invitation to me — that song about sleeping in the desert with a billion stars all around, and when Isaac said that about the stars and the firmament, I was happy for a moment, but a second later I thought of that other desert song, that Neil Young song, "A Horse with No Name," which was popular when Lee and I were married. Lee used to play the guitar and sing that song, and I used to sing along, harmonizing, and when Frieda was little, she'd clap her hands and join in, too, in her own half-intelligible baby talk. She'd stand in front of us and sing, bending her knees to the rhythm. "Horsey No-No" she called the song. Sing "Horsey No-No," she'd say.

A FEW DAYS after Melissa had come over with her spiritual landscape book, a buddy of Lee's came to visit. Lee's friend's name was Denny, and I didn't like him one bit, yet for years, I dared not say anything of the sort to Lee, and whenever Denny came, I tried my best to be the perfect hostess, making big meals of what I thought were manly things, like steak and baked potatoes with sour cream and chives, but inside I was angry. Denny always acted like I didn't exist or as if I were Lee's maid. He was a big guy, and he'd just turn his back on me and talk to Lee, blocking me out not only with his words but with his rude body language. I despised him, but I was nice to him, even flirted with him, just so there wouldn't be any trouble between Lee and me.

Denny and Lee always drank and carried on about old times or talked about stocks and real estate, politics, and airplanes — they both had their pilot's license, and when Denny was around, Lee was meaner than usual. He was never really attentive to Frieda, although sometimes he could be so loving. He would chase her and tickle her and make her giggle like nobody else could, but when Denny was around, Lee acted annoyed by Frieda's very existence. Once, when Frieda was just a toddler and Denny was visiting, I was down in the basement doing laundry, and when I came upstairs, I discovered that Lee had locked Frieda out on the porch as if she were a dog. She was standing there, poor little thing, looking in the picture window and sobbing, and Lee just sat there, slouched in the wing chair, one leg thrown over its arm, nursing a drink, with his back to the window. But Denny, Denny was facing the picture window. There was no way he could have avoided seeing little Frieda out there, alone on the porch, crying, no way he could not have known what Lee had done to her.

This time when Denny came, he brought his fiancée, a beautiful young woman named Yvonne Evanoff. Her last name rhymed with mauve: Evan*auve,* and I loved the sound of it, the spell of it, and all through dinner that night, I kept saying her name to myself like a mantra: *Yvonne Evanoff, Yvonne Evanoff.* And later, after Lee and I had had our fight out on the road, and even later, alone, I couldn't let her name go. It stayed with me like a benediction. That was long ago, but even today, I often find myself saying her name as I lie awake at night or walk down the alley — *Yvonne Evanoff Yvonne Evanoff* — thinking about how I might use it.

Yvonne Evanoff was beautiful but utterly aloof; she hardly spoke the whole time she was there. (She and Denny ended up leaving that same night, rather than staying the whole weekend, as planned.) It was as if she were encased in her beauty like a beetle trapped in a drop of amber. She was tall and fair, with a long, elegant neck and the longest limbs I'd ever seen. She had an impassive face, with full lips and green eyes, and the most unusual color hair — a caramel blond. She must have been Nordic, and she was quite a bit younger than Denny, younger than me, even.

When they got out of the car, Denny walked around and opened the door for her, which faced our porch. First her legs appeared, slowly, as if in a Hanes stocking commercial with Juliet Prowse, and I heard Lee whistle. Under his breath I heard him say, "Holy shit, will you look at that!"

I'd already had a few drinks before they arrived, just because I knew it was going to be a long weekend. Lee had coke, but he wouldn't let me have any. He was holding off, he said, until Denny arrived, which really pissed me off because I knew he'd already done some. You didn't just "have" cocaine without having tried it, and he wouldn't have even told me about it if I hadn't asked. The one thing Lee couldn't do well was lie to me right to my face after I'd accused him of something I knew he'd done.

As Denny ascended the porch stairs, Lee reached out and started patting him on the back, and I said in an affected Beverly Hillbillies' accent, "Well, if it ain't Lil' Dennis the Menace come to see us." I said this in a loud, cheery voice as a joke, but Lee turned to me, and I could see by his side his hand was in a fist.

"Gloria," he said, "why don't you tend to dinner?"

Yvonne didn't come into the kitchen or speak to me at all. Lee made mixed drinks — whiskey sours and margaritas — talking all the while to Denny, and I did my thing in the kitchen: dressing the salad, putting the steaks on the back porch grill, wrapping the Parker House rolls in aluminum foil, steaming snap beans. Frieda was seven that summer. She stayed in her room, coloring, when Denny and Yvonne arrived, although she had helped me earlier snap the beans and set the table.

"Mommy, what's an alcoholic?" Frieda had asked me that day. She was sitting at the kitchen table then, coloring in her Strawberry Shortcake coloring book while I was washing the lunch dishes.

"An alcoholic," I said, turning toward her, "is someone who drinks too much alcohol."

"What's alcohol?" she said, coloring furiously, not looking up.

"Like beer and wine."

"Like what's in our refrigerator?" she asked.

"Yes," I said. "Why?"

"Oh, no reason," she said, shrugging her little shoulders. She was kneeling on her chair, digging through her shoebox of crayons, engrossed in her busywork, so content she seemed, so unconcerned, and I turned back to the sink.

FROM THE KITCHEN, I could see Lee and Denny and Yvonne in the living room. Yvonne sat in the wing chair, her shoes off, her legs curled up. She had a golden tan and her golden hair matched her skin. She was the tawniest person I'd ever seen, the color of a yellow Lab or a palomino. Like Lee, I couldn't take my eyes off her. I kept going to the doorway where I could see her. She was wearing a simple white sheath, structureless, but made of a clingy, crinkly material. Curled in the wing chair, she reminded me of a kind of candy that was a caramel swirled about a white confection, a candy that melted in your mouth and that my father used to bring home in a small white bag and give me as a special treat if I were especially good.

When we sat down to eat, Yvonne still had not spoken to me. It occurred to me that maybe she didn't understand English, and I found myself speaking loudly and slowly to her the way people have a tendency to speak to foreigners. Yvonne still sat there, ignoring me as if she were deaf or I were invisible, and after a few attempts at making conversation, I gave up entirely. I drank my wine and poured myself another glass, and another, and ate my steak and watched the sky turn a magnificent purple, the color of red cabbage.

At some point, Denny said something about going to visit Yvonne's family, and Lee said — I'll never forget this — he said, "It's always good to meet a woman's mother before you make any commitment. If the mother still looks good, then there's a good chance the daughter will hold up, too. If there are any signs of obesity or sagging," he continued, speaking with his mouth full, "then it's best to get out while the going's still good." He took another bite, and I kept my eye on his Adam's apple bobbing up and down, and the vulnerable hollow beneath it.

"Skin, too," Denny said. "Good skin is a woman's passport. Look at Yvonne. Her mother was a model. For Estée Lauder."

"No kidding?" I said to Yvonne, who was sitting across from me, and she nodded and blinked. My own mother had died when I was eleven, six years before I met Lee. Now I was surprised that Lee had "invested" so much in me without having had the opportunity to inspect my mother and calculate the probable maturation of his investment.

"You should see Yvonne's mother," Denny offered. "She's often mistaken for Carly Simon."

While Denny spoke, Lee sat smiling and chewing and nodding. They'd switched to beer now, and Lee took a long pull off his Corona, a slice of lime swimming toward the bottom of the bottle.

At that time I was twenty-seven. I'd given birth to a child and nursed her until she was almost two. I'd had one other pregnancy, also, before Frieda, which had gone almost to term. My already large breasts, once a 32-D, had flattened and spread out to a flabby 38-C, and my stomach was marbled with stretch marks like a good cut of meat. In spite of that, I knew I was still good-looking, but that night, during dinner, I found myself recalling with a strange mixture of longing and repulsion how Lee used to parade me around and praise my physical attributes the way he and Denny were now adoring Yvonne. I remembered Lee grabbing my behind in public, in front of his friends, and making lewd remarks, and how I just laughed and leaned against him, letting him carry on; how I'd always worn clothes that he liked even if I didn't; and how all these years I'd kept my hair long, the way he liked it. I remembered how once, after a few drinks and Lee's urging, I'd told a risqué joke of his at a party, using words I could barely say, and everyone had laughed, but afterward, I had to go in the bathroom and wash out my mouth repeatedly with water. That was so long ago, but the thought of that night still gives me the same sick feeling.

My mother had to have all her teeth pulled when she was in her mid-thirties. I was a little girl then — probably about the same age as Frieda that summer — and I remembered how my mother suffered, how she cried and kept her hand over her mouth so no one could see her toothless before her gums healed and she could wear the false teeth, which were too even and too white. My mother was heavyset, too. All the women in my mother's family had been beauties, shapely when they were young, but "letting themselves go," as my mother used to say, in middle age. They had heavy legs and fleshy upper arms, and after menopause, they developed varicose veins and dowager's humps, slowly evolving into diminished, gnome-like versions of their young lovely selves.

I'd begun to see little dents and lumps of cellulite on my thighs, and two years earlier, I'd given all my bathing suits and short shorts to Goodwill and wore only slacks and skirts, or

Bermudas. Earlier that summer, Lee and I had taken Frieda to D.C. to visit my oldest brother, Frank, and his partner, Bin. We went to the National Gallery, and when we came upon that famous painting by Gustav Klimt, *Danae,* that big painting of the woman with long red hair, curled up in a fetal position, her kimono with the peacock feathers falling open, her left nipple exposed and her thigh, too big, in the foreground like a ham, Lee turned to me and said, "She looks like you, Gloria!" and laughed his ugly laugh. Lee, who used to call me, sweetly, Sister Golden Hair So Bright.

Now, at the dinner table with Lee and Denny and Yvonne, I was three sheets to the wind and seething at this sexist conversation about women and their mothers.

"What about teeth?" I said loudly. "Don't forget the teeth, Lee! And gums! Always pull back the lips and get a good look at the gums!" I said. I tilted back my head and chugged my Chablis and then slammed my glass down on the table, where it hit the edge of my plate and shattered. Frieda darted from the table and ran upstairs to her room, where I found her hours later under the bed. All the while I was talking, I was shaking. After the glass broke, I pushed up my upper lip with my index fingers to show my gums, stood up, stumbled backwards, and fell over my chair, banging my head and spraining my wrist.

That wasn't the first time I'd hurt myself or caused a scene. There was a time a year or so earlier, during an argument, when I pushed over a tall free-standing bookcase crammed with books behind a chair where Lee was sitting. I could have killed him. Or Frieda, if she'd been nearby. Another time, I threw an empty bottle through the picture window, and once, in a motel in Atlantic City, I threw a can of hairspray into the bureau mirror and shattered it to pieces. That was the same trip that ended with me taking Lee's car and his wallet, leaving the motel in the middle of the night with Lee passed out on the bathroom floor, me tearing along the New Jersey Turnpike, still stoned, Frieda sucking her thumb in the backseat.

LATELY, I HAVE been thinking about Lee and Frieda, about my first marriage — a starter marriage, it would be called nowadays — a union based on some wild attraction, a union that everyone except the bride and groom knows is doomed. And most likely, the bride and groom know it, too; they just defy it or embrace it. Thumb their nose at disaster, spit in its face, and marry anyway.

When Lee and I ran off and got married — by a justice of the peace in Maryland where there was no waiting period, no blood tests — we signed some papers, and the said to me, "Will you be changing your name?"

Lee and I looked at each other and burst out laughing. "Better not," we said in unison and laughed some more.

Our wedding night, we had a big fight. I told Lee about an affair I'd had a few months earlier, with Bill at the ad agency, during one of the times Lee and I were on the outs. I should never have told Lee about Bill, but I thought, We're married now; that's all in the past. And I told Lee because I wanted him to know, I wanted him to understand that it wasn't just him who had made a choice. I had made a choice, too. I ended up spending most of our wedding night shivering in the car in my skimpy nightgown. I'd locked myself there to get away from him.

FRIEDA HAS REPEATED the mistakes of her father and me. She has taken out a peace bond against her estranged husband, I've heard, and is fighting for custody of their child, a little boy named Gideon, but I know that neither Frieda nor her husband are fit to raise a child, just as Lee and I were not at their age, at any age.

Lee has been dead now for almost three years. Died in a

small airplane crash, he and three other men, on their way to the annual air show in Oshkosh, Minnesota. He died a wealthy man. He'd made many wise investments, and during the eighties he'd bought up a lot of rental properties, very profitable ventures. He never remarried, but he had lots of girlfriends, always young pretty girlfriends, I heard. He was sixty-one. According to his obituary, his companion was a girl whose mother I know. The girl is about Frieda's age now. She must be twenty-three or twenty-four.

Lee left a good bit of money to Frieda, although she and Julian squandered it all on drugs, I'm sure. It was gone within a few months, and as soon as it was gone, the trouble started. I believe it was that lifestyle that claimed them, that indentured life of addiction where you're reduced to being nothing but a slave to your own body, kowtowing to its insatiable cravings, soothing its howling pains. As if your own body were a bad dog you must keep muzzled and on a short leash at all times.

Live ye not the life of the body, I once heard a preacher holler. It was at a Pentecostal revival in a tent along the river, the place out on Old Indian River Road near Wally Walker's car lot, where the summer circuses and carnivals used to set up. I was in high school then, and three of us had dropped acid and gone. There were rumors of people rolling on the ground and speaking in tongues, and some people said there was a pickup truck with a cap on the back and inside were wooden crates full of copperheads and rattlesnakes, and late at night, they brought them out and "took up serpents" to test their faith.

The ground was wet and smelled like river mud, and we could see the tent's sidewalls wicking up the dampness and patches of green mold growing like psychedelic moss right before our eyes. Thick orange extension cords coiled under our feet. Women with dung-colored hair worn in buns and snoods, their hands folded over white Bibles held on their denim wraparound skirts, sat demurely in the folding chairs. Fat men with dandruff, wearing brown polyester tab pants and dingy white shirts, their faces flushed with fervor, beside them.

We snickered and laughed during the hymns, played badly on a Yamaha electric piano by Sister Dawson. But to this day, I have never forgotten Brother Clifford's words: *Live ye not the life of the body,* he shouted and licked his lips, *for the body will trick you. The body will consume you with its wickedness and evil ways.*

He pointed at me with a chubby, ringed finger, sweat dripping off his jowls, his eyes bright and blazing. But I had already been seduced by the body. Its kiss was on me, black and indelible as the quotation mark tattoo of a rattlesnake's bite. I knew even then I was forsaken, reckless, and wild. But I laughed. I owned it. I laughed in Brother Clifford's red flaccid face, and when the call came for sinners to come forward, come to Jesus, my friend Vinny barked like a dog and crawled up front on his hands and knees to be smoted and saved from eternal damnation.

Sister Glory, Sister Beryl, Brother Vincent we three called each other after that. "Live ye not the life of the body," we'd laugh, passing the hemostat, lighting the bong.

Recklessness was in Frieda too, like it was in both Lee and me. In Julian, too, probably, or else Frieda showed it to him, like Eve extending the apple, and he could not resist. You could see that wildness in Frieda by the time she was eleven or twelve. You could see just a hint of hardness in her sweet face, something powerful lying low in her new body like a jack-in-the-box.

In my top dresser drawer, I still have a picture of Lee and me on the day we eloped. It's taken in one of those Polaroid booths in the back of a Woolworth's, four photos in a strip. We're both laughing, and I look so pretty and happy in those pictures. I look beautiful in those pictures. I look like Vivien Leigh, like she looked when she played Scarlett O'Hara. And Lee looks like a young Robert Redford. I was eighteen; Lee was thirty-five. I had a twenty-two-inch waist when we got married. In fact, it was my waist and hips, Lee said once, which attracted him to me. A few years ago, I read an article in some magazine like *Cosmopolitan,* and in this article, an anthropologist said that a female with a small waist and ample hips "excites the mating instinct in males." That sentence made me sick, but I knew that what that anthropologist said was true.

I used to think it was the combination of big brains and opposable thumbs that was the fatal flaw of *Homo sapiens*. Without that combination, we couldn't very well have come up with so many poisons and weapons, so much bad behavior. But, who knows, really, our human potential?

Lately, though, I've come to think that the flaw in the design of the world is an altogether different biological snafu. It's the frequency of female ovulation. It's too damn easy for most women to get pregnant. Frequent conception made sense in the beginning of time in order to people the world, but whoever set things in motion failed to take into account the exponential population growth, and he or she had on rose-colored glasses, too, if you ask me, and didn't really have a clue about human nature. Noah, I say now as a joke, should have taken two of every species but pulled up the gangplank before any woman set foot on board. If conception could occur only once or twice in a female's lifetime, if ovulation was more like the passing of a comet rather than in keeping with the monthly cycle of the moon, then life would be so much more precious, and there would be fewer of us to fight our wars and do our evil deeds. Children would be worshipped and not be treated so cruelly.

Believe it or not, Frieda's estranged husband, Julian, is related in some complicated way to Lee's old buddy Denny, the guy I could never stand, the guy who was there with his fiancée, the lovely Yvonne Evanoff, that last, horrible night Lee and I were together. It's the kind of coincidence that, if you read it in a book, you'd throw your hands up and sigh, *Oh, puh-leeeese. Cut me a break!* How unlikely, but, what can I say? It's a small world in many ways, and that's the truth. Life doesn't follow the pat rules of fiction.

You know, I should have seen it all along. How could I have been in love with someone whose best friend I couldn't stand? Friendships are telling. Friendships are true. And now here the same character shows up again, so to speak, a variation on the same theme, in my own daughter's life. It's creepy. It's that six degrees of separation thing, how we're all linked one way or another, if not by blood, then by attraction, choice. Maybe by some kind of marking or destiny — like Blue Indigo and her tribe — or maybe just by chance. Whatever. It seems that each generation just acts out the same old stories, assuming the familiar parts. Relentless repetition, like that old Bible verse says: *What has been is what will be, and what has been done is what will be done; there is nothing new under the sun.* Another gem from Bill's cubicle, his take on the boring repetition of advertising.

How sad it is to see Frieda following in my staggering footsteps. And her boy, Gideon, what kind of man will he grow up to be? Will he end up hating his mother — and other women — like Frieda seems to hate me? I often think about what that psychic Miss Donna down in West Virginia told me: my Frieda will survive. That prophesy sustains me.

Frieda's husband, it turns out, is something like a second cousin to Denny or a second-cousin-once-removed. Whatever that means, I can never remember.

Removed. That's such a funny word for it.

La Vecchietta in Siena

SURELY IT WAS IMPOSSIBLE, but nevertheless, somehow the old woman had followed LaRue all the way to Italy. The first time LaRue spotted the old woman was in the bus station near the Piazza Santa Maria Novella in Florence. LaRue was standing in line to buy tickets for herself and Nash to travel to Siena to see the fourteenth-century frescoes by Simone Martini. LaRue was especially interested in seeing *The Miracle of the Child Falling from the Balcony,* in the Church of Saint Augustine; the Duccio angels in the Museo dell Opera del Duomo; and the birthplace of Saint Catherine of Siena, who at the age of six received a mystical vision of Christ, a few years later, the stigmata, and soon after that, miraculously learned to read and write. And there, behind the ticket counter window, was the old woman.

Both LaRue and Nash had been taken by the slides of the City of the Virgin, as Siena was called, which Fanny, their tour guide, had shown the previous night. Siena — only an hour's bus ride from Florence — was a medieval town with cobbled streets and beautiful buildings built of stones in soft hues of

browns and pinks, ochres and lemons and olive greens. Some of
the buildings dated back to the twelfth century. There were cathedrals with frescoed walls and ceilings, Moorish stripped pillars, and pink and green marble floors — wonders of architecture that had taken centuries to build. And today was the day of
the world-famous Palio, a magnificent medieval pageant culmi-
nating with a bareback horserace in which seventeen horses rep-
resenting the seventeen different *contrade,* or districts of the city,
raced around Siena's central square, the Campo, competing for a
coveted banner honoring the Virgin Mary, Siena's patron saint.

Today was the only "free day" on the six-day Tuscany art
tour LaRue and Nash were a part of, a day when everyone was
on their own, a real treat after so many hours in the constant
company of strangers, some of them obnoxious and pretentious,
and not one of them a person Nash or LaRue could connect
with. They'd never do it again, sign up for a tour. LaRue, in
particular, loathed the way they had to follow the tour guides
around. Claudia — the younger guide, the second-in-command
— carried a gaudy, plastic sunflower on a telescoping rod high
above her head, so everyone in the group could spot her in a
crowd, and none of them would get lost. They all followed her
like a herd of old sheep, heels click-clacking on the cobbles like
hooves. LaRue felt ridiculous, but Nash was able to look past the
nonsense and just soak up the art.

A troop of children on a field trip is what it felt like to
LaRue, each of them with a nametag bearing a large sunflower
and contact information pinned to their shirts, so that if they got
separated from the group they could be escorted back to their
hotel on Via Della Scalla, which was only a few blocks away
from the Duomo, Florence's tallest, most visible, most famous
landmark, an enormous cathedral with a magnificent dome any
nincompoop could spot just by looking up.

LaRue was indignant about the mandatory sunflower IDs,
pointing out that she had navigated through life for over sev-

enty years and adding that she also spoke Italian. (Although, if the truth be known, she didn't. She could sing the choruses of "Volaré" and "O Sole Mio," and years ago she had an album with Maria Callas singing the arias from *La Traviata,* which she used to sing along with, but that was the extent of her self-pro-claimed fluency.)

"No exceptions," Fanny said cheerily, simply dismissing LaRue's objection and continuing to elaborate on the other tour agency rules concerning punctuality and group courtesy.

"Will we all earn badges for tour etiquette?" LaRue called out as a joke, but no one laughed, and Fanny and Claudia ignored her. Nash nudged LaRue with his elbow, and even though she didn't look his way, she could feel his disapproval trying to penetrate her peripheral vision, and she felt like crying. Lately, she'd been blurting out what she thought instead of keeping it to herself like she'd done all her life. She didn't know why she was doing it, and often after she said something dispar-aging or sarcastic, she was depressed for days, and she vowed to keep her mouth shut, but before long it happened again.

Although Fanny was the one in charge of the tours, Claudia was the smart one, LaRue determined, the one who really knew her stuff about medieval and early Renaissance art. During the walking tours, Fanny moved ahead of the group, wearing black tights, a short black skirt, a smock-like black jacket with a gored back and big cuffs, and a black beret, an outfit that LaRue — who favored bold, bright colors — thought so affected and so ill chosen for a middle-aged woman, a woman with a big behind. She should change her name as well as her wardrobe, LaRue thought, managing not to say it out loud.

Fanny would be posing at the entrance to cathedrals and mu-seums when the tour group arrived. She'd give an introductory lecture on what they were about to see, then Claudia would take over, herding the group along with her sunflower, pointing out and elaborating on details that Fanny had only mentioned. Fanny would disappear and show up hours later at their next destination. LaRue could do without her and her big butt and brash red hair, no doubt out of a bottle.

Nash's knee was bothering him again, and so he sat on one of the green metal benches out on the bus platform, reading the *International Herald Tribune* while LaRue waited in the long line at the bus ticket office. She could see Nash through the glass doors, folding and reading the newspaper in the neat manner she always admired — the way commuters read papers — folding them into a rectangle no bigger than a slim gift box for gloves and holding the paper in one hand while they stood, the other hand holding on to one of the bars or a strap suspended from the ceiling, as if on a merry-go-round.

Having read the newspaper his entire life every morning and evening on the commuter train, Nash was attentive to not only the news but to its presentation, and how things were continued from column to column, page to page. There was an art to it all, a formula for continuation that made a newspaper easy for folding and reading, and Nash was often outraged when a continuation deviated from that template and required unfolding and folding the paper again, an unforgivable waste of time, an infraction.

LaRue never read the news. She was sick of newspapers and their propaganda. She read the obituaries, "Your Daily Stars," "Dr. Gott," and the weather report, and sometimes she would work the word scrambles, but she wasn't as good at them as she used to be. Time was when LaRue could get the word scrambles almost immediately, without thinking really, just by squinting at the jumbled letters until the correct word appeared, like those pictures that look like a mess of dots, but if you stare until your eyes cross, Seurat's *A Sunday Afternoon on the Island of La Grande Jatte* or a waving American flag comes forward in 3-D. It was almost miraculous how LaRue used to be able to "see" the correct words in the word scrambles, and Nash often said that if there were a scrambled-word quiz show on TV like the old *Password,* why then LaRue would be champion and they'd be millionaires. But anymore, the word scrambles just made LaRue anxious. Stare as she might, no words came forward.

ICARRCLU. That's an easy one, but LaRue had puzzled on that word jumble for nearly an hour the other day as they toured the Uffizi Gallery, closing her eyes and trying to picture the word instead of looking at the da Vincis and Botticellis while Claudia did her spiel. And yesterday's *International Herald Tribune*'s bonus word, UNTUBFLISAM, had her awake past midnight, drawing in the moonlight with her index finger as the ceiling fan in their hotel room wobbled and stirred the air and Nash snored away.

LARUE STOOD WITH her shoulder bag on one arm, wearing her passport and wallet in a pouch around her neck, as Nash insisted, because she was always losing things. Setting things down and then walking away. The day they were leaving on their trip to Italy, LaRue had left the book she was reading in the beauty shop. The worst thing was that she was on the next to last page when Janice called her for her wash, rinse, and cut, and she set the book down on a stack of magazines while she slipped on the plastic cover-up. Once she'd returned home and couldn't find the book, Nash insisted that she call Makin' Waves even though LaRue remembered having the book in the car on the way home. The book's dust jacket was very distinctive — a detail of the Lascaux cave painting of a bull and horse — something you couldn't really miss if it was sitting right there on the seat next to you, LaRue said.

And so Nash made the call himself, and sure enough, that's where the book was, at Makin' Waves. LaRue wanted to go back after it, but Nash said absolutely not, there wasn't time to drive back across town. Their flight was at five P.M., they had to be at the airport to meet their group by three, and it was already noon — and the airport was an hour away in the opposite direction.

And so the vacation to Italy was about to begin on a bad note, LaRue in one of her moods, the end of the book eluding her like so many things in life had: a college degree, children. It was a book of short stories and the last story, the one LaRue was reading, was about a foal born prematurely during a subzero night in some godforsaken place like Idaho or Montana, and now LaRue couldn't rest, not knowing whether the poor little thing had lived or died. LaRue loved horses and had been quite a good rider when she was young. She was a natural horsewoman, people said. Nash's family had two quarter horses back then, and LaRue had even taught riding lessons for a few years when she and Nash were first married.

While Nash was boiling himself an egg, LaRue took the cordless phone and slipped into the powder room under the back stairs to call Makin' Waves herself. The receptionist, Tess, was a perky little thing with blue hair and multiple piercings, and when LaRue explained the situation, Tess said just what LaRue had hoped she would: "Let me read it to you, then, so you'll know."

Three times Tess pronounced *foal* as a two-syllable word, something like *fo-all*, which annoyed LaRue to no end, but she managed not to correct her; she listened carefully and thanked Tess and hung up the phone quietly, and then she couldn't stop crying. The end was not what LaRue had expected. The foal had lived after all, but it was a miracle that it had, and LaRue knew that even though it had survived birth, Life was going to take its toll on the poor little thing, and Death would never take its eyes off of it.

When Nash knocked on the powder room door and called her name, LaRue pulled herself together, sniffled, and splashed some cold water on her face, concealed the phone in her pocket, and answered brightly, "Just a minute."

LARUE WAS READING another book as she stood in line at the bus ticket window. A tiny man with a big nose and a red cap like Johnny Philip Morris sat behind the counter, and when LaRue was almost to the window, she glanced up from her book and was startled by a glimpse of the old woman standing behind the little man on the other side of the glass. At first LaRue didn't recognize the old woman. She stared for a moment, and the old woman stared back, and then they both looked away.

"How much she looks like Aunt Bertie," LaRue thought.

The old woman looked different from the last time LaRue had seen her — when that was she couldn't say. It could have been months. The expression on the old woman's face was so alarming — like a migratory bird that had lost its sense of direction. What was the old woman doing in Italy? Her hair was a steelier gray and shorter now, cropped into an uneven and unbecoming pageboy that ended at an awkward midear length, making her look like a parody of Buster Brown or like Jonathan Winters impersonating Little Lord Fauntleroy. The old woman wore glasses, too, with black and silver frames. The same as Aunt Bertie's? And a purple bucket hat!

Lately, the old people had been appearing to LaRue — the dead people like her parents and her Aunt Bertie, Uncle Stanley, her brothers Dorsey and Reggie, and even Angry Jack, her curmudgeon grandfather who came from the old country and lived with them when LaRue was a little girl. At first, LaRue was frightened by these apparitions, mostly because she recalled stories of terminally ill people seeing visions of long-dead relatives come to help them cross over, and LaRue feared that her number was about up. Although she had been raised Catholic and attended parochial schools, she had pretty much abandoned the

faith by the time she was graduated from St. Anthony the Abbot
Catholic School for Boys and Girls. In college, she declared herself an agnostic and her faith Missourian: "Show me," she said,
"and I'll believe it."

When it came right down to it, LaRue didn't know what she
believed about death and the spirit, about a life everlasting, but
experience was neither affirming nor reassuring. Never had she
had any out-of-body experiences nor any visions of anything out
of the ordinary. Until recently, that is. These visitations from the
dead were not unpleasant, though; in fact, they left her feeling almost exhilarated, as if she'd received a mild electrical
shock. They were brief, very casual manifestations, always when
LaRue was alone. She'd walk into the kitchen and there would
be her mother in her bib apron, peeling potatoes at the sink; or
LaRue would look out the kitchen window and there would be
her father walking from the vegetable garden toward the back
door, holding two ripe tomatoes. These ghosts — if that's what
you'd call them — never spoke or made eye contact, but instead
vanished in a split second. It was probably just her imagination.
No need to mention any of this to Nash.

On the flight from Munich to Florence, however, LaRue had
seen her father on the plane. She was heading up the narrow
aisle, returning to her seat after using the bathroom, and there
was her father standing in front of the curtain that separated the
tourist class seating from the business class section, just two rows
up from LaRue and Nash's seats. It was her father, all right,
looking spry and healthy, just as he had looked before the operation. A shock of white hair, exemplary posture, plaid Wool-
rich shirt, big smile. He was looking right at LaRue as if he
were about to speak, and he wasn't wearing the strip of flannel
around his neck like he had had to wear after the tracheotomy.
He leaned forward with his hand on the back of the seat just in
front of Nash. Surely Nash saw him, too. It had to be her father

or some doppelgänger . . . but no . . . Nash *didn't* see him. How could that be? And when LaRue was only a few steps away, her father disappeared. Poof!

Nash stood and LaRue settled into the window seat without a word. Far below them, through the mist, the Alps spread out in a great ragged sweep as far as LaRue could see. She had expected the Alps to be totally snow covered as she'd seen in movies with mountain climbers or skiers, but from the air, the Alps looked black, black as the Pennsylvania culm piles, with only the peaks covered in snow. The long mountain ridges rose up like the backs of wild boars between deep, pinched valleys. The whole mountain range reminded LaRue of a delicious dessert her mother used to make: a glass bowl of Nabisco Famous chocolate wafers standing on edge, with whipped cream spooned over them and set in the freezer, a dessert called Snow in the Mountains.

Nash leaned over LaRue and looked out the window, too. How desolate it all looked.

"Hannibal of Carthage," Nash commented, "crossed the Alps in 217 B.C. with an army of thirty-eight thousand soldiers, eight thousand knights, and forty elephants, to conquer Rome."

How could that be possible? LaRue stared down at the black, perilous landforms, and gradually, through the filaments of clouds, she could make out the mountain passes like black satin hair ribbons, and then she saw them: the pale gray masses weighted down with provisions, the horses no bigger than seahorses, the ant-size troops, the great procession stretching and winding like a charm bracelet, mile after mile, disappearing behind one mountain, then reappearing in front of another.

Staring down at the Alps, LaRue recalled a story a neighbor — a woman named Rosa — once told her about fleeing Germany in the nineteen-thirties. They had gotten a car from somewhere and were escaping from the Nazis into Switzerland — Rosa and her sister and her sister's four children. Rosa was the only one who knew how to drive, and as they were crossing the Alps at night, a terrible blizzard began. In no time at all, the narrow, already treacherous road was covered with ice and snow, and the snow was blowing about so willy-nilly that Rosa couldn't see past the car's Pegasus hood ornament. They were all shivering and terrified and praying, even the little children huddled in the backseat, praying and whimpering. They were creeping down a slippery mountain, skidding and sliding, when they saw her — the Virgin Mary — up ahead. She was dressed in her pink robe and blue mantle, hands out, palms up, in the classic lawn-ornament pose, with a pinkish, fish-tankish glow like a neon outline all around her. Rosa slid to a halt and rolled down the window.

"Rütsch mal," the Blessed Virgin said, opening the car door, *"ich kann fabren."* Scoot over and let me drive.

Rosa moved over on the bench seat, next to her sister who was holding the youngest child, a baby named Harold, and the Madonna climbed in and took the wheel. When the compartment light came on as the door opened, Rosa could see that the Virgin Mary wore thick black stockings underneath her gown and black rubber-soled shoes with a chunky heel. The Holy Mother sped through the mountain passes, shifting gears like Parnelli Jones, handling the car as if it were a Ferrari. Just before the German-Swiss border, their car was waved through a roadblock by a Gestapo officer who never even stepped outside, just stuck his arm out a window into the sleet, and they never even had to show the forged documents that identified them as French citizens, not German Jews.

Once in Switzerland, the Virgin Mary stopped the car and disembarked. She walked into the headlights, spread her arms and legs like someone about to be frisked, and then shot up into the air a few feet like a bottle rocket. She paused a moment, midair, to make the sign of the cross above the Duesenberg, and then dove off the side of the mountain like a hawk after a rabbit.

It was a remarkable story Rosa had told, one that LaRue had relished and retold many times over the years, often embellishing it for the sake of story and to make people laugh. How wild and fantastic it seemed; why would the Virgin Mary — a Catholic saint — come to the rescue of a carful of Jews? But now, from thousands of feet above the Alps, looking down through the clouds, LaRue could almost see the black car inching its way through the snowy mountain passes like a flea, Rosa's anxious face behind the wheel, and LaRue knew for sure that Rosa's story was true, and she regretted her mocking renditions of it. Why *shouldn't* the Holy Mother come to Rosa's rescue, was the real question, not why *wouldn't* she. Mary was, after all, a Jewess herself. Her husband and son: Jews, also. God, the father, was the only one whose religious affiliation was up in the air.

It will come to pass in the last days, it says some place in the Bible, LaRue recalled from her catechism classes years ago, *that I will pour out a portion of my spirit upon all flesh. Your sons and daughters shall prophesy, your young men shall see visions, your old men shall dream dreams.*

Maybe it wasn't so crazy after all.

When Rosa told LaRue her story, her hands and voice shook, her teacup rattled, and her eyes shone brightly from where she sat across LaRue's kitchen table, describing the blizzard in great detail. Like a "snow wreath," she called it, like the terrible journey of Gerda, the little girl who traveled through a world of ice and snow to retrieve her friend Kai from the evil Snow Queen's ice palace. Rosa described the forged documents in their leather portfolio. Rosa stomped her foot on the linoleum floor, shaking the kitchen table, to make the sound of soldiers' boots marching down the streets of Stuttgart. That was years ago when Rosa told her story, and now LaRue couldn't recall if Rosa was the one driving or if she was the sister holding the baby or maybe one of the children huddled in the backseat under an eiderdown.

LaRue barely knew Rosa, and for Rosa to tell LaRue — out of the blue — this bizarre tale thrilled LaRue but frightened her, too. From then on, she was a little wary of Rosa and avoided hanging or taking down her own wash when Rosa was at her clothesline; LaRue knew Rosa was some kind of crackpot. She'd heard other stories about her. About how she'd once brought a pot of stone soup to a covered dish dinner and how she dressed her little boy like a girl, and how people said she carried on conversations with squirrels and groundhogs, dogs and crows.

Speaking of animals, humans weren't the only apparitions LaRue had grown accustomed to seeing. Their first night in Florence, LaRue awoke in the middle of the night having to pee, and after using the lavatory, she walked to the casement window, pushed open the shutter slightly, and looked down into the courtyard three stories below. There she saw two gleaming eyes, and as her own eyes adjusted to the darkness, she made out the figure of a dog, a black dog sitting underneath the fig tree in the center of the courtyard, looking up at her window. The dog looked so much like her old black Lab, Lucille, who had died six months earlier, so much so that LaRue had to go down into the courtyard and see the dog, maybe pet it. Nash was sleeping, so LaRue slipped on her red raincoat and took the room key and crept down the cement stairs in her bare feet. She stepped into the courtyard, and the dog came running to her, wiggling and wagging its tail. It was Lucille!

IN SIENA, A light rain was falling, and throngs of people hurried down the steep streets toward the Campo, children deliberately slipping and sliding on the slick cobbles. LaRue and Nash followed the crowds and found themselves climbing the steps to a cathedral where they were pressed through the massive blue doors by the hordes of people behind them. There were no pews or seats inside, and what seemed like thousands of people were crushed into the nave, leaving only a narrow aisle cordoned off down the middle. As more and more people entered, LaRue and Nash were pushed farther forward. Hundreds of candles illuminated the dark interior, and colored streams of light from the stained glass windows poured in from high above like spotlights at the Ice Capades.

LaRue and Nash had no idea what service they were attending. There was no way to leave; they were packed into the cathedral as tightly as beans in a guessing jar. All around them, people whispered in Italian and then, after a long time, they heard the resounding clip-clomp of hooves on the marble floors. Silence engulfed the cathedral as quickly as if someone had just accidentally sat on a television's remote control, activating the mute function.

Down the central aisle pranced a parade of magnificent horses, wearing colored plumes and elaborately embroidered blankets like the steeds of medieval knights, each horse led by an altar boy in a white surplice. A priest, resplendent in gold-embroidered vestments and purple miter, appeared, surrounded by more altar boys swinging thuribles of incense. The horses snorted and stomped, and the priest blessed each animal as it paused at the altar before being led out a side exit. From her childhood, LaRue recognized the cloying fragrances of frankincense, myrrh, and Damascus rose. The smell made her nauseous. She tasted the sour vomit rising like sap in her throat and held on to Nash, leaning against his arm to keep from swooning.

Above the altar, Duccio di Buoninsegna's Virgin Mary, with her seasick green face, looked down forlornly at the crowd. LaRue recognized her immediately, recalling Fanny's explanation for the Virgin's Kermit the Frog face: some ingredient in Duccio's secret recipe for flesh color had caused his paint to oxidize peculiarly over hundreds of years, rendering Mary's original peaches-and-cream complexion more amphibian than human. Off to Duccio's Virgin's right, among a throng of frescoed angels with gleaming coronas, the old woman in her purple bucket hat looked down, too, and sort of waved.

IN THE FRESH, damp air outside the cathedral, LaRue recovered. Now at the Campo, as time for the Palio approached, the crowd grew rowdier with each passing minute. The race begins at a corner of the square where all the horses are penned behind a rope; a free, riderless horse charges the group from behind, and the race is on. During the race, a horse that throws its rider is still eligible to win, and some of the horses even begin the race without jockeys. Beyond the finish line, the horses continue running, racing out of the Campo and through the streets of Siena in all directions, pursued by frenzied spectators. Last year at the Palio, a drunk had reeled out onto the track and been trampled, a child had fallen from a balcony overlooking the plaza and been killed, and a number of people were severely injured after the race, during a stampede.

The steady drizzle continued, and LaRue shivered underneath her red raincoat in spite of the thousands of bodies packed around her. The crowd moved en masse, pressing LaRue and Nash against the ropes that contained the spectators within the inside circle of the track. Suddenly the horses took off, their hooves thundering through the Campo. Only a few seconds into the race, a riderless horse, a magnificent bay, slipped on the wet cobbles, stumbled, and went down right in front of LaRue and Nash. The horse struggled to get back up, straining his neck and kicking his legs, two other horses almost colliding as they leapt over him. LaRue let go of Nash's arm and slipped under the rope. Before anyone could stop her, she put her arms around the horse's gleaming neck and climbed onto his back as he rose to his knees and then was off again, galloping around the track, gaining on the other horses, overtaking them by twos and threes. LaRue rode bareback, holding on to the horse's mane, her red coat flying out behind her like a mud flap, her purple bucket hat trampled on the track far behind.

Up ahead, the coveted banner bearing a billboard-size image of Duccio di Buoninsegna's Virgin had been raised above the finish line, and LaRue reached out with one hand to touch the Madonna's prodigious pink and green cheek. Under the banner, off to one side, LaRue's father and mother stood cheering, her mother in a floppy-brimmed straw hat, their arms laden with bouquets of white roses and peace lilies. LaRue's big brother Reggie was there, too, smiling and holding a horseshoe made of flowers, and her sister, Bernadette! And there was her brother Dorsey with Lucille on a leash beside him. Lucille smiled and barked and wiggled in a way that Nash had long ago dubbed the "full-body wag."

"Vai, vecchietta!" the crowd roared. *"Avanti! Vai! Vai!"*

Go, old lady! Go on! Go! Go!

"Viva la vecchietta! La vecchietta, oo-rah!"

Acknowledgments

The following people made important contributions not only to this book but to the way I read, think about, and write stories: Brandy Vickers, Gail Galloway Adams, Mark Brazaitis, Peggy (Moojiburr) Andreas, Beth Nardella, Ethel Morgan Smith, Cheryl Torsney, Jane Vandenburgh, and Kevin Oderman. Thank you also to Reem Abu-Libdeh, Sabrina Bindocci, Nermina Zecirovic, Deborah Janson, Tracy Roe, Victoria Hartman, Christopher Moisan, Jenny Bent, and Houghton Mifflin Company. And to Mary and Harriet, thanks, respectively, for the wild party and the rat.

ALSO BY SARA PRITCHARD

CRACKPOTS

A New York Times Notable Book
Winner of the Bakeless Prize for Fiction

"A powerful novel, beautifully written. Sara Pritchard illumi-
nates the significant moments in her characters' lives with
compassion, elegance, and wisdom."

—**URSULA HEGI**, author of *Stones from the River*

When we first meet Ruby Reese, she's a spunky kid in a cow-
girl hat, tap dancing her way through a slightly off-kilter
1950s childhood. With an insomniac mother and a demo-
litions-expert father, her entire family is what the residents
of her small town would call "a bunch of crackpots." Sara
Pritchard's remarkable first novel guides us through Ruby's
life, between childhood and adulthood, from past to present and back again, with humor and melancholy, imagination and insight.

ISBN-10 0-618-30245-X
ISBN-13 978-0-618-30245-1

Look for the reader's guide at
www.marinerreadersguides.com.